DYING FOR LIKES

KILLING AIN'T A GAME

ARYANNA

LOCK DOWN PUBLICATIONS AND CA$H PRESENTS

Lock Down Publications

P.O. Box 944

Stockbridge, GA 30281

www.lockdownpublications.com

Like our page on Facebook: Lock Down Publications

www.facebook.com/lockdownpublications.ldp

STAY CONNECTED WITH US!

Text **LOCKDOWN** to 22828 to stay up-to-date with new releases, sneak peaks, contests and more…

Like our page on Facebook:
Lock Down Publications

Join Lock Down Publications/The New Era Reading Group

Visit our website:
www.lockdownpublications.com

Follow us on Instagram:
Lock Down Publications

Email Us: We want to hear from you!

DEDICATION

This book is dedicated to Shatavia Lakia because you were there when it happened.

ACKNOWLEDGEMENTS

First and foremost, I give all glory to God for allowing me to still possess this gift, even though I take it for granted sometimes. I'm thankful for my fans, who have grown with me over the years and remained loyal despite my faults. Just know that the best is yet to come. I wanna thank my family for being family, especially my sister, Big Byrd. Your son, Marcus, is lucky to have such a wise and caring mother, and I'll be there to remind him of that when he's going through his shit as he gets older. To my kids, I pray that you know that I love you all regardless of our differences. Special shout-out to Asaiah, aka Peanut! I love you, and you won't see this until you're old enough! Lol! Ayo, Pooh, welcome home, my nigga! Shamyiah, I fuck with you, even though you be acting light skin all the time! And JJ, if you don't go sit your thick ass down somewhere! Lmao! Shout-out to my real ones locked behind the g-wall. Keep that dirt off your name, fam, because your rep can make or break you on the inside. Shout out to Noodles and the whole Richmond Highway! You bamas can be from Alexandria, but that don't mean you from the Highway! Meadow Woods stand up! Shout-out to all my ops too because I forgive you for being you. Lol! Just remember that if it ain't life, it ain't long. Before I forget, shout-out to my family and supporters out in Leesburg. I'll see you soon. LDP 4 Life!!!

1

JANUARY 2025

Death had a certain smell to it in its finality, and it was not one you'd ever forget once it had rode the airwaves through your nostrils to your brain. The same could be said about the smell of sickness. When I opened the front door to my mother's ground level apartment, my nose was immediately filled with a stench that tossed my mind backwards to the time I'd spent in the hospital as a child. I'd been there to get treated for a few gunshot wounds, but the smell of sickness invaded my pores like it was the fragrance applied to my hard hospital sheets.

For days, I laid in that hospital bed, breathing in the pungent aroma of the different diagnosed ailments floating around me, until the power of death overpowered it. All it took was seventy-two hours for me to internalize a smell that my memory was now recalling to the surface twenty-five years later. At forty years old, relatively fit and healthy, I felt more vulnerable than that bullet riddled fifteen-year-old because the smell of sickness I was now forced to inhale was more personal. It was personal because it was coming from my own mother. I closed the front door behind me and stood still for a moment while I mentally checked to make sure my emotions were concealed in their proper place. By reputation, I was a gangsta, block tested and hood approved, but I was still my mom's baby boy, and to see her sickly hit me different. I wasn't too hard to cry, but I didn't wanna upset her, and so I always stepped to her with my bravest face on.

"Nathan, is that you?"

Her voice was weaker than it had been when I was a kid, and she was telling me to get my Black ass in the house, but it was still recognizable to my soul, and it made me smile.

"Yeah, Ma, it's me."

"Bring me a bottle of water on your way back here," she demanded gently.

"Yes, ma'am."

I put my keys in my pocket while turning left and stepping into the tiny kitchen. Knowing that she probably hadn't eaten made me decide to fix her a bowl of fruit quickly and carry it to her with the bottle of water. As I walked down the hallway, heading to her bedroom in the back, the smell of my own fear for her health stronger and stronger. With each step, I steeled myself to withstand the pain I always felt at seeing her in her current condition.

"Good morning, Mommy," I said, giving her a smile that felt like it had been painted on with nails.

"Hey, baby, what's going on?"

"Same old shit, just figured I'd check on you before I headed to work," I said, taking a seat beside her bed.

"I'm fine, Nathan, and I told you about worrying so much over me."

"As I remember it, I believe it was you who sat beside every hospital bed that I've ever had to lay in. Since you *refuse* to stay in the hospital, I'mma sit my ass right here and worry about you as much as I want. Now stop fussing and eat something," I replied, preparing to feed her the fruit if necessary.

"I don't have a appetite, and if you even *think* about forcing me to eat, I'mma show you that I can still whoop that ass."

I stared at her for as long as I could keep a straight face, which didn't last long because the look in her eyes was deadly serious. Once I started laughing, she joined in, and a smile touched her face and transformed her features into the woman I'd known my entire life —_if only for a moment.

The cancer had knocked so much weight off of her that she would forever be a shell of herself, but that light in her dark brown eyes was fierce when the flame was lit. That light had always made her 5'2", stocky frame seem more dangerous than Iron Mike Tyson in his prime. Marcela Ty was a fighter to her core, and she'd passed that gift along to her kids, which was why we rarely ever let the game of life beat us. I didn't know how to fight the inevitable enemy that was Father Time though. That muthafucka was undefeated and had no weaknesses to exploit, and that left no good options other than acceptance. I hadn't figured out how to do that yet either.

"Here, drink this," I said, untwisting the top off the bottled water before grabbing her straw off of her nightstand.

I held the bottle in front of her and waited while she drank as much as she could handle. Ordinarily after a couple of gulps, she would let up, but by the time she pulled back, half of the water in the bottle was gone. The way that instant color sprang into her cheeks confirmed my suspicion that she was dehydrated.

"Mom, when was the last time you ate or drank anything?"

"Well, it's been a couple of days since I ate, but that's because I didn't have an appetite. I had something to drink yesterday when your sister, Bridgette, came over."

"Why didn't Yah Yah check on you last night or this morning before she went to school?" I asked, frustrated.

"She's with her boyfriend, and I think she spent the night at his house."

"Since when is it okay for my seventeen-year-old sister to be laid up at some nigga's house?" I asked heatedly.

"Since her mama was confined to a bed, her big sister took over as director in her corporate job, and her big brother became a little obsessed with world domination through entrepreneurship."

When I opened my mouth to clap back, I caught myself and paused a moment so that I could hear the harsh truth in what my mother was telling me. We were all preoccupied, and I knew that a big part of that was that we were running from the painful truth of our mother fading away. None of us wanted to truly look this death in the face with her, but denying the reality didn't make it any less real.

"I'm sorry, Mom. I won't make excuses for any of us. I'll just say that we all need to do better."

"Oh, I know that, but *you* have to be the one who gets through to your rock head sister of yours," she informed me.

We'd all inherited our mother's stubbornness to a degree, but my thirty-five-year-old sister, Bridgette, and I had learned to mellow out enough to listen to reason. Yah Yah was still smelling herself and thought she knew all the answers before the questions were even asked.

"I'll make time to talk to her, but that's a problem for later. Is the marijuana no longer helping with the nausea and keeping your appetite up?" I asked, setting her water down on the nightstand and sitting back down.

"Yeah, it helps, but I'm all out, and Bridgette didn't have any. Yah Yah probably does, but like I said, she ain't bring her little ass home."

I pulled out my phone to check the time to try and guess what class Yah Yah would be in because it would be faster to link up with her than drive back to my house in Maryland. It wasn't that my mom's spot in Alexandria, Virginia was far away from mine; it was the morning traffic that I was sure to run smack into. I sent Yah Yah a text, letting her know that I needed some good gas and that I could link up with her now. While I waited on her response, I decided to broach a new subject with our mother.

"You know, Ma, I make pretty good money, which means I can afford to get you an in-home nurse."

"Sure, just make sure he's got a big dick and he knows how to use it," she replied, smiling.

"Ewww! Mom! Cut that shit out!"

"Well, that's what you get for suggesting dumb shit, fool. I don't need nobody's nurse up in here, smoking all my damn weed, eating my food, and trying to tell *me* what to do. I'm grown, Nathan, and I'mma die that way. You understand?"

"Mom, I get it, but this ain't working. So, either you get a nurse or you come live with me like I've been asking for the last year."

"Live with you? And how will your wife feel about that?" she asked sarcastically.

"It don't matter how she feel because that's my house and you're my mother. Those are two undeniable truths, so what's your next question?"

Before she could respond, my phone pinged and alerted me to a new message. I scanned it quickly, mumbled in frustration, and then fired a text back.

"You okay, son?"

"I'm good, Ma. I'm just gonna whoop your daughter's ass when she gets home from school," I replied, shaking my head.

"Do I even wanna know why?"

"It's no big deal. I just gotta go meet her connect, who happens to be her boyfriend," I stated.

"Oh, she's a brave one to put you two in the same room."

That was my thought exactly, but the man-to-man talk would have to wait until later because I was pressed for time. I had exactly forty-five minutes before meeting with my liquor distributor, and I had to close that deal in order to start getting shipments into my clubs and restaurants. My mother hadn't been exaggerating about my quest for world domination through business, but *nothing* came before family. The next ping going off on my phone provided me with an address and instructions to bring the cash. The prices started at $800 an ounce. I immediately responded that I was willing to pay $5K for a pound, and I was on my way.

"Mommy, I'll be back. I'm going to get you something to smoke, and I'll get you some food while I'm at it."

"Okay, baby, thank you. I'm just gonna take a little nap until you get back," she replied softly.

Within seconds, I heard her breathing get deeper as her chin connected with her chest. I sat there and watched her for a second before pushing myself up out of the chair and heading for the door. I could feel my heart hammering against my ribs as I fought back the tears that were biting the back of my throat. As a secure man, I didn't have an issue with crying, but I did have one with feeling sorry for myself. So, I kept my tears in their rightful place as I headed outside. Once I slid behind the wheel of my black 2025 BMW 951i, I was able to take a calming breath and recenter myself. I hit the push to start, turned up the Lil Baby leaking through my speakers, and moved out. After stopping at the bank, it only took me fifteen minutes to pull up in front of an apartment building known as the Sex House, but it wasn't as rundown as I remembered. The actual name of the building was the Sussex House, but with all the drugs and pussy that had been pumped out of that place since the early 2000s, it had earned its nickname. The grayish bricks that had held the old building up had been replaced by glass and steel, giving it a modern look of somewhat improved taste. I shot a text, letting Yah Yah know I was here, and a few moments later, she told me to go around to the west side entrance to meet someone named Flacco. For a split second, I hesitated because I was torn between what was politically correct and what my instincts said. Most niggas got nervous when someone showed up with a gun to buy product, but my experiences dictated that I didn't go anywhere foreign unarmed. After a few more seconds of contemplation, I hit the button on my stereo to flip down my flat screen so that I could scan my palm. Once my palm was recognized, my trunk popped, and I got out to retrieve my Ruger .45 out of its hidden lockbox. Tucking the pistol into the waist of my gray slacks, I made sure my black button up was covering it, and then I headed toward the building. As soon as I rounded the corner, I spotted a tall, slim built, Black dude smoking a cigarette, leaning against the building. I approached with confidence but was not arrogant enough to appear threatening.

"Flacco?" I asked.

"Yeah, follow me," he replied, tossing his cigarette and opening the side door.

I followed him inside and up one flight of steps before we came to a door where he knocked three times. The door was pulled open by a cute Spanish chick who immediately stepped aside and let us through. I swiftly noticed that the apartment was decorated more like a model home than a trap house, and the other two Spanish chicks dancing to music in the middle of the living room were more beautiful than the one who answered the door. Growing up in the streets, I'd run into a lot of bad bitches with bad habits, but none of these gave me that vibe. There was only a faint hint of weed in the air. I observed all this in a matter of seconds without breaking stride, but I could feel my brain nudging something in my subconscious just beyond my reach. Still, I kept moving forward and avoided eye contact with any of the women so that there wouldn't be any ego tripping over somebody else's woman. About halfway down the hall, Flacco stopped and tapped on the door to his right before pushing it open. I didn't hear what he said to the person inside, but he motioned me forward and stepped out of the way. When I got to the door, I stopped, locked eyes with Flacco for a second, and in that moment, I felt that nudge again in my mind. Feeling it once could be explained, but twice couldn't be ignored. Just as I was preparing to make up an excuse to nullify the transaction, my peripheral vision caught movement. When I glanced to my right, I saw a teenager standing in the middle of the bedroom floor, cradling an AR-15 with a drum on it, smiling at me.

"Your money or your life," Flacco said.

2

"Are you sure that this is what you wanna do?" I asked softly, looking Flacco squarely in the eyes.

"I'm positive, and unless you wanna die, then I think giving up the money is what *you* wanna do," Flacco replied, pulling out a chrome Glock .40 and pointing it at my head.

I could tell that the Glock had a switch on it which would allow him to empty his extended clip in a matter of seconds after tapping the trigger. Both of the guns pointed at me equaled bad math if I tried to reach for my own pistol, so my best option was to comply with the demands being made.

"I'm reaching in my pocket to get the money," I said, moving slowly.

"Smart move. Now toss it in the bedroom," Flacco directed.

I raised my arm with the same slow, deliberate speed, and I launched the stack of money in a high arc toward the kid in my peripheral. Everything seemed to happen in slow motion, but I immediately saw the tables turn. When the teenager extended his right hand to the sky to catch the money, he was suddenly holding the AR-15 with one hand, almost as if it was an afterthought. That was the first mistake. The fact that Flacco's eyes shifted to follow the trajectory of the money was the second mistake, and as soon as it happened, I made my move. My left hand locked on the Glock's barrel, while my right fist shot out with enough speed and force to snap Flacco's head back. I twisted the gun loose from his grip and hit him with another short jab while using the momentum to move forward out of the line of the shooter in the bedroom. In one swift move, I maneuvered my body behind Flacco and smacked him over the head with his own pistol. As he was sliding to the floor, barely conscious, I saw the barrel of the AR-15 announcing the teenage shooter's intention to step out on me. I raised the Glock in his direction to fire at him, but all I got for my efforts was the resounding click of an empty chamber. By the time I dropped the gun and upped my own pistol, the barrel of the assault rifle was almost winking at me, but I felt no pressure. The ice that had flowed through my veins since I'd witnessed my very first execution took hold, and I could feel the smile tugging at my lips right before the bullets flew. Brain matter and blood instantly decorated the hallway wall like an expensive abstract painting, courtesy of the kid with the AR.

"Wait-wait, Nate. It's not that serious..."

"But it is though," I said, taking aim at Flacco as he tried to get up off the floor.

I put two bullets in the back of his head before training

my gun on movement that I spotted at the end of the hallway. My eyes locked with those of the Spanish girl that had let me and Flacco into the apartment a short while ago. I expected to see fear or shock, but her brown eyes held mild amusement instead, and something about that stopped me from shooting her. Instead, I grabbed my money from the dead teenager's pocket and ran back toward the front door. When I got right in front of the Spanish chick, she stepped aside while pulling the door open for me. I never paused in my escape, but my brain was trying to make sense of the fact that the other women were still dancing in the living room like nothing had happened. By the time I made it back to my car and had it racing out of the parking lot, I was calm enough to realize that nothing that had just happened made any fucking sense. After setting the autopilot feature on my car, I pulled my phone out and immediately called Yah Yah. Her phone only rang once before going straight to voicemail, which signaled that she was in class. My thought process was that she could possibly be in danger now too, and until I knew more about the niggas I'd just killed, I had to get her somewhere safe. I sent her a text message, telling her to be out front of her high school in ten minutes because I was coming to get her, and then I called Bridgette. I anticipated her phone going to voicemail, but I wasn't about to leave her a detailed message that could be used later. I told her to call me right the fuck now, and I hung up.

When I took the car off of autopilot, I pushed the gas pedal to the floor and watched the speedometer jump to ninety miles per hour. In and out of traffic, I weaved, leaving behind a trail of blaring car horns accompanied by angry shouts and middle finger salutes. I was seconds away from coasting through a red light when I spotted a cop car sitting in a McDonald's parking lot three feet away. I was going too fast to stop, which left me with the only other option of swinging a hard right that had the back end of my car twerkin. I spared only a glance in the rearview mirror, and when I didn't see any flashing lights, I put my foot back down hard on the gas pedal. Having to take a detour added an extra two minutes to my route, but I still slid to a stop in front of Mount Vernon High School nine minutes after the shooting had taken place. I grabbed my phone off of the seat and called Yah Yah again.

"Fuck!" I exclaimed in frustration when her phone went straight to voicemail again. The thought to send her another text message crossed my mind, but I wasn't about to waste any more time. My next decision involved whether or not I was gonna try to walk into this school with my gun on me. Given what had just happened, it was undeniable how real the threat was, but metal detectors had long since been the requirement at the entrances to all schools across the country. I debated for a few more seconds, and then, I put my hand back on the screen so that my palm could be scanned, and my hidden lockbox reopened. Once I got out of the car, I went straight to the trunk, stashed the gun, and headed for the school's main entrance. As soon as my hand wrapped around the door's handle, an alarm started blaring from multiple hidden speakers.

I had no idea what this meant, but I knew that it wasn't good. Before I could pull the school door open, a metal gate slammed down directly behind the glass, which effectively blocked my view of the school's interior and stopped all forward progress. I felt my pulse quicken as my heart beat faster, and the panic within me tried to rise from below the surface. Knowing that my little sister was more than likely the target of whatever was happening beyond this metal barricade was increasing my helplessness and feeding my anger. These feelings quickly made up my mind about my next move because I was bow determined to get in by any means necessary. I turned to go back to my car, but I only got as far as the sidewalk before a swarm of red and blue lights had me boxed in.

"I need to get inside the school because my sister could be in danger-."

"Freeze! Hands up!" the cop yelled, pointing his gun at me.

"Listen, I need to..."

"Hands up NOW, Ty!" he yelled again.

Knowing how easily a misunderstanding could happen with a trigger-happy cop forced me to put my hands up and stop moving toward him. It wasn't until I was reaching for the sky, looking down the barrels of multiple weapons, that I realized that the first cop who had spoken had used my name. I was sure that I didn't know him, and I hadn't been in legal trouble for years, which meant that him knowing my name was another issue altogether

"My hands are up, and I'm not resisting," I stated slowly and clearly, looking at each officer's body cam.

"Get down on your knees and lace your fingers behind your head."

This demand came from the same cop who had addressed me by name. His name tag said Gaines, and I quickly committed his features to my memory so that I'd never forget him or this moment in time. He stood about an inch and a half over my 6'2", but my two hundred seventy pounds dwarfed his barely there one hundred eighty-five pounds. The look in his flat brown eyes gave me the impression that he'd burn my ass happily in broad daylight if I gave him half a reason to. His bald head, light skin complexion, neatly trimmed goatee, and thick ass glasses gave him a nerdy Boris Kojo vibe, but it was obvious that Officer Gaines was homosexual. Not even a gun in his hand could hide his feminine side, and the slight smirk that I detected made me think that he enjoyed telling me to get on my knees in front of him.

"Am I under arrest, Officer?" I asked calmly.

"You damn right you are, and if you don't get on your knees now, I'll have to interpret your actions as resisting arrest," Gaines replied seriously.

There was no doubt that he was threatening to shoot me, and I didn't believe for a second that it was an idle threat. So, for the second time today, I did what I was told. Officer Gaines never took his weapon off of me while two other cops cuffed me and roughly threw me into the back of a cop car. Before I could get the first question out of my mouth, another cop hopped into the driver seat of the cruiser, and I was whisked away.

The rage that I felt continued to grow around the idea that I was being unjustly arrested for some bullshit, but in the pit of my stomach, I knew real fear. The fact that I was called out by name as soon as the cops pulled up was what had me stuck with more questions than answers. I didn't say shit though. I simply kept my cool and waited. Fifteen minutes later, I was inside a windowless police interrogation room, sitting across from two detectives in matching dark blue suits. Nobody was talking, but I knew this was a play to see who would break first. After about five minutes of an intense staring competition, one of the detectives pulled his phone out and began scrolling away. I almost laughed at their little ploy until he flipped the phone around and slid it across the table to me. As soon as I looked down, I saw a kid's head exploding from a gunshot, but that wasn't what gave me chills. That feeling came from watching me double tap Flacco.

"Nathan, we have you for murder, two counts to be exact. Any questions?"

3

"Questions? Nah, I only wanna talk to my lawyer, so I'd appreciate if you could get me a phone as soon as possible," I stated politely.

"You sure that you don't wanna give us your side of the events that took place on film because a case could be made for self-defense."

The sincerity in the cop's tone irritated me because he was lying convincingly enough to trick the average muthafucka, but I wasn't that. I was a nigga who had battle scars when it came to the criminal justice system, tried and true like food stamps on the first, so they could miss me with the bullshit. They had video footage of what went down with Flacco, which meant that they saw me shoot a nigga in the back of the head, and there was not a single argument for self-defense that could be made when that happened. Talking with these muthafuckas had no advantage for me, and we all knew that.

"Does your hearing work in a way that allows you to

hear in a different language but respond in English? Because I said I want a *lawyer,"* I stated firmly.

The frustration was easy to read on the cop's face, and even though it gave me some small pleasure, my mind was otherwise engaged on trying to assess the mess that I was now caught in. The cops exchanged a look that voiced their frustration through the silence, and then they stood up.

"No matter what lawyer you get to defend you, the results will remain the same. You're gonna die in prison."

"Does that mean that you won't visit and write?" I asked sarcastically.

The flush of anger heated their cheeks before spreading across their faces and changing their white complexions into something resembling a constipated baby. Past experiences had taught me that the angrier the police got, the more dangerous they were, but I was just as dangerous in high pressure situations. Neither man said anything else before leaving me alone. With the resounding click of the door closing behind them, my mind shifted gears, and the questions began flowing throughout my brain. I knew that the video footage was real and authentic, but what I wanted to know was how the fuck it had gotten in the hands of the cops within ten minutes of the shit going bad. The only thing that made sense was that there was some type of setup in motion, but even that still didn't make total sense because it would mean that Flacco wanted to die. If not, then he'd intended to film the robbery, which would've landed him in the seat that I was occupying had I not turned the tables. It just didn't add up, any of it, and especially not the unexplained way the cops got the footage. I sat, enveloped in complete silence, searching for the piece of the puzzle that I was most certainly missing. After about ten minutes, the door to the small, windowless room opened, and in walked a fresh-faced patrol officer with a cordless phone in her hand. She didn't say a word; she simply handed me the phone and pressed her back against the nearest wall. I ignored her presence and quickly dialed my sister, Bridgette's, number while praying that she answered this time. After seven rings, I was preparing to hang up when my prayers were answered in the form of her voice booming in my ear.

"Nate, what the fuck is going..."

"There's no time to explain. I'm in police custody in Alexandria, and I need a lawyer down here asap," I said, speaking rapidly.

"What's the charge?" she asked.

"Murder, two counts."

I heard Bridgette take a deep breath, and I could feel her anxiety radiating over the airwaves.

"Sit tight, bruh. We'll be there in a minute," she said, disconnecting the call.

When I hung up, I was intending to give the cop the phone back, but I found myself dialing Yah Yah's number again. It rang three times, and then I heard my little sister's voice.

"Nate?"

"Yah, are you okay?" I asked, feeling somewhat relieved.

"I'm-I'm fine. I'm so sorry, Nate. I swear to you that I didn't know that shit was gonna get that crazy."

I opened my mouth to express my joy that she was

alright, but something was suddenly tickling my subconscious and causing me to listen to her words clearer.

"Y-You know what happened?" I asked.

"Yeah, everyone knows because it's all over Instagram, but bruh, it wasn't supposed to go down like that, I swear on my life."

What she was saying was making no sense at first, but then I got a sick feeling in the pit of my stomach. I didn't wanna have this conversation over an open phone line while I was in police custody though. My curiosity and paranoia would both have to wait for the satisfying relief of whatever truth my sister knew.

"Yah Yah, I need you to listen to me. I want you to go home and stay by Mom's side until either me or Bridgette call you. Do you understand?"

"Yeah, but Nate, you gotta believe me..."

"Yah, I do believe you, but now ain't the time for this conversation. You heard the automated recording when you answered this call, so you know that the cops are listening. Anything that we need to discuss can wait until later, but for now, I need you by Mom's side and nowhere else. Lock the door and set the alarm."

"The alarm?" she asked, sounding surprised by my words.

Anyone listening would've thought that I was referring to some aftermarket ADT system designed to alert the authorities should someone break in. Yah Yah knew different though, and she knew that I was telling her to get my AK-47 from under the floorboards in my old bedroom so that she'd be ready. Even though I had no idea what was going on, the fact that I'd taken the lives of two young niggas in the street meant that there was some type of street consequence coming. I didn't know who either of these niggas were associated with, but no civilians lived in the Sussex House apartments. There would be some blow back behind what I'd done, and I didn't need my family paying the consequences for my decisions. This was all on me.

"I got you, bruh. I'm headed for the house right now," she replied.

"Good. I need you to make a couple calls as soon as you get off of the phone with me though. I want you to call Stucky and tell him to be on the next thing smoking from Atlanta. Tell him to move quickly and quietly. Then, I want you to call my wife and tell her to come down to the jail if they give me a bond. Can you handle that?"

"Yeah, bruh. I'll do it right now. I love you," she said.

"I love you too," I replied, hanging up and holding the phone out toward the cop.

She took it without saying a word and left the room as quietly as she'd came. My instructions had been simple enough, and they'd sounded innocent of the true motive behind what was already mentally taking shape in my mind. My little brother, Stucky, was three months younger than me, so he was really my twin with the same daddy and different mom. We had a lot in common, including the savage ruthlessness that we embodied when us or someone we loved were threatened. We were old niggas according to the streets, but we'd achieved that success by shedding the blood of our ops in a merciless fashion. Me sending the message that he needed to move quickly and quietly let him know that it was time to go to war. One of the fundamental principles that he and I valued was that there was no time to argue or negotiate peace when war had been declared, and despite not knowing everything that was necessary for me to give a full assessment of the situation, I knew that more people would need killing sooner than later. Stucky would agree, but my wife, Shytavia, might not be as under-standing or eager to burn parts of the world into the ground. I knew that her loyalty to me was above being questioned though, and she would follow wherever I led —even if that took us both to hell. For the moment, I still didn't know where I was leading us to, but now that I'd set things in motion, I turned my mind back to Yah Yah and what she'd been about to confess. At first, I'd just thought that she was expressing the guilt she'd felt because it had been her nigga that had made a move against me, but now, I was almost certain that she meant something way different.

If I didn't know any better, I would've sworn that my own sister had set me up to get robbed, but the loyal side of me refused to believe that. No sibling relationship was perfect, but ours was a long way from the amount of hatred it would take to inspire that type of betrayal. Still, her words had to mean something, and her contrition seemed genuine enough to make me believe that somewhere along the line, she'd fucked up. That was a problem but only one of many. The other immediate problem was that somehow, the murder had ended up on Instagram Live. Ultimately, I knew that it would be taken down, but the question was how the fuck did it get up there to begin with? My mind immediately went to the three women who'd been in the apartment, seemingly oblivious to what was going on in the back of the apartment, and the oddness of their behavior again stuck out in my mind. The music hadn't been too long to drown out the gunshots, but they hadn't panicked in the slightest. Shit, one of them had even opened the door for me on the way out! I'd thought that was weird then, but now, everything was being looked at through the lenses of suspicion, and it wasn't adding up to anything good. It crossed my mind that one of them had to have shot footage of the robbery gone wrong, but the angle of the camera from the video on the cop's phone meant that whoever filmed it would've had to have been in the hallway and the bedroom. If any one of the females had been that involved, I would've dropped the hammer on them without hesitation, and the girl who opened the door for me didn't have anything in her hand to film shit with. The only other option was that the cameras were in place before I got there, but that made even less sense. Before I could analyze any further, the door opened, and the two cops came back in followed by a slender, Black man wearing an impeccably tailored suit.

"Marcus Devareaux, esquire," he said, extending his hand toward me.

I shook his hand while giving him a silent appraisal, but I already knew that he had to be good because my sister wouldn't have sent him otherwise.

"Okay, Mr. Ty, now that your attorney is present, let's talk about..."

"My client and I would like to confer alone please," Marcus said, moving to stand between him and me, which made our position even more clear.

I didn't say anything, and I managed not to smirk despite my overwhelming desire to do so. The cops left without argument, which surprised me, but their actions were the least concern on my growing list of concerns.

"Bridgette sent me," he said, turning to face me.

"How much do you know?"

"Assume that I know nothing and start from the beginning," he replied, taking a seat across the table from me.

I quickly ran down the details, sticking to only what was known because, despite being in a privileged conversation between my lawyer and I, I still didn't trust these surroundings. When I finished speaking, he sat there quietly for a moment and just let the situation sink in.

"Have they taken you to the magistrate to see about bond?" he asked.

"No, they just tried to get me to confess to the crime by offering up the possible argument of self-defense."

"You should've admitted it," he said seriously.

For a second, I looked at him like he was crazy as fuck, and I was already planning to cuss my sister out, but there was something about the supreme confidence in his stare that triggered my curiosity.

"Self-defense won't play in court when a man is shot two times in the back of the head," I stated dryly.

"True enough but we're not going to court for this."

His tone carried with it a weight of finality that I found comforting even though I didn't understand where his confidence was coming from.

"Feel free to let me in on your little secret because from where I'm sitting, this situation is way more serious than you're making it out to be," I said.

"Okay, how about I spare the theatrics and just show

you what's behind the curtain?" he said, standing up and going to the two-way mirror.

He waited for me to nod at him, and when I did, he tapped gently on the glass. A few moments later, the two cops from earlier reentered the room.

"I want my client released immediately and his car returned to him with the same speed that you're gonna use to take his handcuffs off," Marcus demanded.

"That ain't happening in this lifetime," one cop said, smiling.

"Well, unless you have body cam proof, or any type of footage, to show that you read my client his Miranda rights, then I'd say that you'll be releasing him fairly quickly. Unless you wanna actually take this to the magistrate judge and have him laugh in your face," Marcus said, smiling.

Neither cop uttered a word, but the expressions of fear on their faces was unmistakable, and it filled me with hope. I hadn't even realized that my rights hadn't been read to me, but Marcus had obviously reviewed the footage of my arrest and listened closely to me recounting the details. I didn't know what his going rate was, but if this move that he was trying to pull actually worked, then I was damn sure gonna pay him double. The silence in the room was thicker than cigar smoke in a gentleman's club until three firm taps sounded off from the other side of the two-way mirror. The instant slump in both cops' shoulders spelled out dejection as they turned to leave the room, but no part of me felt sorry for them.

"I'll go with you," Marcus said, giving me a sly wink before following them out of the door.

All types of thoughts tried to push their way into my

mind, but my focus was locked in on my imminent release and the consequences that would carry. Even if I never made it into the open courtroom behind what I'd done, I knew that the court of public opinion still wouldn't be kind to me for what happened. It was one thing to shoot someone in self-defense, or to even shoot them down in cold blood, but it was entirely different when there was video footage of it. Getting off due to a technicality wouldn't give me my life back, and until I knew the whole truth, I didn't know that there was anything that could make this straight again. What this would do to my businesses would have to be the last thing on my list to worry about because my first concern was my family. I needed to talk to my wife because my instincts were telling me that she was on her way down here whether she knew I had a bond or not. Shytavia wasn't a product of the streets, but she knew enough muthafuckas who came from the mud to know just how bad this shit was. She was loyal, so I never questioned whether or not she was war ready, and her unwavering support had kept me sane since the moment I'd met her. Today was a different kind of day though, so I knew that she'd show up thinking at least five moves ahead of these slow ass cops. I sat in silence, moving different strategies around my mind for the longest thirty minutes of my life until the door opened, and a new cop stepped in with my lawyer in tow. This cop weighed in for the fight because his build was very close to my 6'3", two hundred seventy pounds, and the muscle definition was clear to see under his dark blue t-shirt. His eyes were a piercing dark brown, and when they locked with mine, I saw the animal in him that he kept caged.

"Nathan, this is Detective Anthony Lashaun, but you may know him by his street name of..."

"Cujo," I said, nodding slowly.

I'd never met the man in person, but his reputation rang out in the streets as the top gang cop in all of Virginia. His base of operations was typically Washington D.C., even though he answered to the governor of Virginia, and the rumors were that he moved like that to ensure that anyone gunning for him would be handled federally. From what I'd heard, his opinion was that Virginia's version of the RICO law was watered down and a joke, so every case that he built, he was aiming for the federal indictment. Our swords had never crossed because I wasn't a gang member or an affiliate. I was all about the money because that made understanding my loyalties crystal clear. For us to be in the same room right now was definitely a bad sign, but I gave no outward appearance of distress.

"Nathan Ty, your reputation precedes you. Not many men make it to forty years old doing the things that you've done without the protection of a misguided army to keep your head in one piece. I must admit that I'm impressed," Cujo said.

"I'm just a humble businessman, Mr. Lashaun, so there's really nothing to be impressed with," I replied.

"You can save the stonewalling tactics for the Feds actually assigned to investigate you. I'm just here to warn you, and I'm only doing that because you inadvertently saved my life," he said.

"Did I? I assure you that it wasn't intentional, but I'm curious nonetheless."

"That's a story for a different time and place, but if you

somehow manage to survive the next seventy-two hours, I'll consider telling you the details of your unintentional heroics. For now, I suggest that you focus," he said seriously.

"What do I need to focus on, Detective?"

"You killed the wrong kids, Nate, so it's not *what* you need to focus on; it's *who*. If I were you, I'd dig a hole, get in it, and pull the dirt in behind me," he replied.

"That's not really my style, Detective."

"Oh, I'm well aware, which was why I wanted to tell you this in person before you left. You're gonna die... and so is everyone that you love in this world."

4

The fact that Cujo's declaration was lacking in tact and professionalism weren't the reasons that his words didn't sit right with me. It was the deadly serious look in his eyes that caused my hackles to raise and my ears to pin back on my head like an attack was imminent. A number of questions flooded my mind, but I took a quiet moment to sift through them before I opened my mouth to gauge the threat.

"Who did I kill?" I asked, raising my hands and affixing an expression of innocence to my face.

"Does the name Ant Troell mean anything to you?" Cujo asked.

"Nope."

"What about Lamborghini?" he asked.

"Do you have a year and model to go with that?" I replied sarcastically, chuckling softly.

Cujo didn't laugh with me. He just kept staring at me with eyes that were well versed in seeking the truth behind the lie. I met his unwavering gaze until a slow smile spread across his face, forcing me to look away because now we both knew my truth.

"Flacco was Ant's nephew, and J-Roc was his cousin. You already know that Ant is known as Lamborghini Lyve in the streets, and he's one of the founding members of the Valentine Blood movement. His power is respected across the country, but it's his business acumen that makes him one of the most feared men in the world. His online private securities firm is used by entertainment royalty like Jay-Z and Taylor Swift, which is why he's not in the streets anymore. He'll never forget where he comes from though, and he's Camden, NJ to his soul. When he left the hood, he brought his 'day one' niggas with him, so the loyalty that he gives those closest to him is unwavering and rarely seen anymore. His little cousin and nephew that you killed weren't part of the gang life, but they were close enough to it to rap about it believably. They were close enough to Ant to know the ins and outs of the streets and being related to him gave them street cred that helped their records sell. Ant is bound by loyalty, which means that somebody is gonna pay in blood," he stated seriously.

"And I'm supposed to be the one that pays? If you ask me, Ant can only be mad at himself for not teaching them niggas that playing in the street could get them hit by a truck. The street ain't made for everybody, and sometimes, even standing on the curb can get you smacked."

"Be that as it may, you killed the wrong people. From what we've been able to gather, Flacco and J-Roc set you up for it to go on Instagram Live and *look* like a real robbery in their music video. Because you've got a reputation in these streets as being somewhat of a renegade who's untouchable by even the most powerful organizations, you would've given them unimaginable clout on social media," he said.

I was listening to his words intently as I was shaking my head, but the head motion was related to what Yah Yah had been saying on the phone. I wasn't 100% sure of what her part was in all of this, but given the fact that this was her nigga, there was no way that this was a coincidence. I could figure all that out later though. Right now, I needed to mentally engage in the potential of an unintentional war because Cujo was right about at least one thing. I'd killed the wrong people.

"Am I free to go?" I asked.

"Are you sure that you wanna leave?" Cujo retorted.

I chuckled softly, but my eyes never swayed from his face.

"If you know me then you know that I ain't never been scared of a little contact, and I'm sure that Ant knows that too."

"That attitude won't save you or your family," he replied.

"Only God can do that either way. Now, am I free to go?" I asked again slowly.

His stare was intense, but it didn't move me.

"Your paperwork is being processed as we speak," Marcus said.

"Thank you, Counselor. And now, gentlemen, this conversation is over," I said, leaning back in the chair.

Everyone paused for a moment, and then Cujo slowly rose to his feet and headed for the door.

"I'mma give you some free game, Nate. Don't underestimate Ant in the slightest because I promise you that he's smart enough and ruthless enough to put your whole family on the six o'clock news. You don't want my help, so I won't offer it. My suggestion is that you get your affairs in order, make sure your insurance premiums are paid up, and pick out everyone's plot of land to be buried on," he said.

Before I could reply, Cujo was exiting the room, never once glancing back at me. When it was just my lawyer and me, he took the seat next to mine, which allowed us to speak quietly.

"How much of what he said was true?" Marcus asked.

"Enough for me to put you on permanent retainer for a while just in case I end up fighting murder charges... again."

"Make sure it looks like self-defense," he whispered.

I nodded once in understanding, which prompted him to get up and leave the room. I spent the fifteen minutes waiting alone, contemplating my next series of moves now that the puzzle was coming together. By the time the cops returned to take the cuffs off of me, I knew what my next play was. Marcus met me in the booking area where my personal effects were returned, and I was directed to get my car from the impound lot around the side of the building.

"Thanks, Marcus, I'll be in touch with your retainer sooner than later," I said, putting my phone and money into my pockets and keeping my key fob in my hand.

"Your sister paid me, so we're good for now, and we can set up billing when it becomes necessary."

I nodded, but I still dug the $5K back out of my pocket and handed it to him, then I headed out the door. The brightness of the sun was blinding, but my eyes were full of bloodlust for a reckoning anyway, so I didn't even blink. When I got to my car, I wanted to immediately make sure that my gun was still in the trunk, but I knew that only a fool would do that here. I got beyond the wheel and quickly exited the parking lot, careful to maintain the speed limit even though I wanted to smoke the tires.

My eyes steadily scanned the rearview and side mirrors, looking for signs of the cops following me. The fact that I wasn't seeing anyone didn't make me feel better because, in my mind, that only equated to cops already hacking into my car's GPS. I was fond of this car, but my mind was swiftly made up that today would be my last day driving it. When I pulled up at the red light, I was thinking about where I could get rid of the car at, so I was partially distracted, but I still caught sight of the all-black, windowless, Ford panel van that came to a tire screeching stop directly in front of me. Because my way forward was blocked, instinctively my hand hit the gear shift, which threw the car in reverse. Just as I was preparing to hit the gas, the side door to the van slid open, and two assault rifles popped out like beautifully naked strippers with big titties. I felt my car rocket backwards as I stomped on the gas while ducking as low as I possibly could to avoid being hit by the bullets now ripping through my windshield. A quick flick of my wrist turned the steering wheel to the right, and gravity did the rest by swinging my car broadside in a 180° spin. Bullets rained like thundering hail from the sky, but my focus was on straightening the wheel back out as I threw the car into drive and fled. Running wasn't my natural inclination, but it didn't make me a bitch; it made me smart. The street nigga in me wouldn't let me go back in the direction of the police station, like I needed them to save me or something. Instead, I hit the nearest corner and raced up a side street at eighty miles per hour. When I looked in the rearview mirror, I saw that the black van was giving chase, but the V-12 under my hood was putting more distance between us with each second. By the time I hit my third side street, I couldn't see anyone behind me, which allowed me to reduce my speed so that I didn't get pulled over by the cops. As I made my way into downtown Alexandria, I made the mental adjustment because my plans had definitely changed due to what had just happened. Cujo had obviously been telling the unvarnished truth, but i hadn't really doubted him because I knew Ant's reputation. Did I think that he would've moved his offense so quickly considering that it had only been a few hours? Hell nah! But it was obvious now that nigga had shooters on speed dial and could call them up like Door Dash. If he thought that he was the only one who had juice like that then that nigga was lost in a delusion where he was the only superpower. After ten more minutes of evasive driving, I pulled up at a McDonald's on Richmond Highway and hopped out. My movements were casual as I went to my trunk to retrieve my pistol, and then, I headed into the restaurant after tucking the gun in my waistband. I ordered a combo meal that I had no intention of eating, sat in the back where I could observe without being observed, and then I pulled my phone out to make a call.

Only a few words were spoken before the call ended, and then I quickly disabled my location on my phone so that I was invisible to those trying to track me that way. I sent Bridgette a text that said one word. Hide. Despite no longer being in the streets, we were from the streets, and that had engrained instincts into us that necessitated an escape plan be ready at all times. I knew that when Bridgette got that text, she would drop everything, get our mother, and go to a predestined location. Given how wild Yah Yah had gotten since she'd become a teenager, it had already been decided that if something like this were to happen, then I would go get her to safety. Given what had happened the last time I'd pulled up at her school, I wasn't even about to attempt that shit twice, plus I doubted that she was still there anyway. If she'd done like I told her, then she'd be at home, protecting our mother, which meant that she could go with Bridgette when she showed up. As I sat in the back of the McDonald's, my eyes roamed everything I could see inside and outside, and as soon as I spotted the black-on-black GMC Denali pull up, I made my move. Leaving the untouched food on the table, I got up and headed outside to the SUV idling next to a soccer mom's minivan. I hopped in the passenger seat, and we pulled off.

"You okay, boo?" Shytavia asked, reaching her hand across the console toward me.

I waited until our fingers were locked together before I took my first deep breath and found some semblance of peace in the chaos. My wife and I had no secrets, so I knew that I was gonna have to tell her the latest, but first I needed to focus on a loose end. I pulled my key fob out of my pocket and pushed the button to lock my doors three times before holding it down for a slow count of ten. Once I released the button, the deafening sounds of an explosion reached my ears.

"Babe, what the fuck?" she asked, jumping as she looked out of the back window at the fireball that used to be my car.

"It's a long story, but I'll start at the beginning," I replied, using my shirt to wipe my prints off of the key fob before tossing it out of the window.

"Where are we going?"

"Underground because I'm definitely on someone's kill list," I said, pulling my phone out of my pocket.

"You say that shit like it's no big deal, Nate, but you promised that I wouldn't lose you to the streets."

I could hear the pain and worry in her tone without looking over at her beautiful face, and it tore at my heart. I'd made my wife a great many promises when we'd gotten married, and I had every intention on keeping them, but to do that meant more people would have to die. I was okay with that, but I needed her to be okay with that.

"Sweetheart, you're not gonna lose me, but there are things that I have to do in order to prevent that. Let me explain what happened first, and you just listen while you drive us to pick up our son," I said, turning sideways to face her.

She didn't let my hand go, and I didn't pull back from her because her strength would make my words flow freely. Given the time of day and our location, I figured that it would take an hour to get to our son, Peanut's, private daycare. That would give me plenty of time to kick that real to her. I didn't have to explain my past in the streets, but going back in time was necessary to explain how I knew Ant. Once upon a time, him and I had been fucking the same girl, who later turned out to be his baby's mama, so that was where the animosity began. I kept that part brief because the goal wasn't to trigger my wife's insecurities. Shytavia was one of the most beautiful big girls that got ignored for the skinny bitches that were shallow, but I'd never ignored her. From the moment I'd first laid eyes on her at one of her cousin's barbecues, she'd had my undivided attention, and I knew that I had to make her mine.

It took me a whole year to give us a real shot, but neither of us had any regrets about it, and we were going on year five now. Still, I knew my wife, and I knew how she felt about my whorish ways from the past. So, I kept it cute about that part and then explained the rest of what had happened this morning when I'd went to buy my mom some weed.

"That shit is crazy," she said, shaking her head once I'd finished running it down to her.

"Shit, you're telling me. When I seen the video, I almost shit on myself, literally, because I just knew that there was no way out, and I was about to lose you and Peanut forever."

"Baby, Asaiah is your son, and I'm your wife, and *nothing* changes that. Okay? Just tell me what we gotta do next," she replied, squeezing my hand reassuringly.

Before I could respond, my phone started making all types of noises in my hand as my notifications started sounding off. I was content to ignore it, but my wife's phone started doing the same thing, and that made my stomach drop. I knew that she couldn't check her phone because she had one hand on the steering wheel and the other still entwined with mine, so I checked my phone. At first, I couldn't make sense of what I was seeing because everyone I knew was sending me what looked like the same new Instagram video. When I finally opened it, I saw my mother's beautiful brown face staring defiantly at whoever was holding the phone and filming her.

"What is it, boo?" Shytavia asked.

I couldn't answer, couldn't even utter a word. All I could do was watch in horror as my heart hammered in my chest.

"You muthafuckas don't scare me," my mom said in a tone laced with venom and hatred.

"We're not here to scare you... We're here to up the score."

I couldn't see the person that she was talking to, but I was trying to focus on the voice in case I heard it again. The loud gunshot that rang out shattered my focus though, and what I saw next allowed my phone to slip from in between my fingers.

5

"Baby... Baby, what happened?"

When I looked over at my wife to try and formulate some type of answer to her question, I could barely make out her face through my unchecked tears. Without hesitation, Shytavia pulled onto the side of the road, and then she pulled her phone out.

"Oh, my God... No," she sobbed a few seconds later.

I felt her arms go around me as she pulled me to her, but I still couldn't see through my tears. I had no words to speak, and the pain that I felt was so intense that I had to shut my mind to it in order to stop the screaming in my head. I'd started this day with the knowledge that my mother was dying slowly, and I'd barely been able to face that. Seeing her executed with the same coldblooded disregard that I'd used on Flacco and J-Roc wasn't something that I knew how to accept or deal with. I was trying with all my might to think of something, *anything*, to make this make sense, but for one of the few times in my life, I couldn't put two thoughts together that could stop my heart from bleeding. I held my wife close, closer than I ever had any other human being in my life, and in that moment, the feeling of her beating heart sustained me. For a split second, my brain stopped its free fall, and an image of innocence pushed into my mind with enough force to make my breathing harsher.

"Peanut!"

"Wh-What, babe?" she asked, pulling back and staring at me.

"We need to get to Peanut. Now."

I saw the fear instantly manifest in her brown eyes, and it translated into swift action as she turned back to the steering wheel. We shot back into traffic, almost colliding with a fast moving eighteen-wheeler, but she avoided the accident and drove like her life depended on it.

"Where's your gun?" I asked, already opening the glove compartment and riffling through it.

"Center console, boo."

I immediately shifted my focus to that location, and within seconds, I had her all-black Glock 9mm in my grip, wishing that I had a target within my sights to unload it on right now. Before Tay and I had gotten married, she never would've been the type to ride around with a gun on her, but after I'd patiently explained my past and the ops' inability to forgive and forget, she'd understood my insistence for her being armed. It would always be better to have it and not need it then need it and not have it. I quickly checked the clip to make sure all fifteen bullets were there, ready to be well placed in a nigga's skull. When that was done, I laid the pistol in my lap and picked up my phone that I'd dropped. As much as it was gonna rip my heart out, I knew that I had to watch the video til the end to see what I could learn. The amount of comments of shock and horror that I saw posted in response to the video only increased the amount of guilt that I was drowning in, but I pushed through it. I said a silent prayer that I wasn't about to witness Bridgette and Yah Yah's execution too because that would simply be more than I could take. I manipulated the video until I saw my mother's vacant eyes staring at me while her blood and her last thoughts leaked from the hole in her forehead. Something in my soul whispered that at least now she was at peace and no longer suffering, and that gave me the fortification I needed to keep watching. Thankfully, there were only a few more seconds before the screen went black, and I was able to let out a small sigh of relief. My intention was to now call my sisters, but my eyes drifted back to the comments on my Instagram. It wasn't just shock and horror anymore because someone had made the connection between me and my mother, and they were calling it instant karma. The fact that there were muthafuckas actually agreeing with this shit had me twice as determined to shoot and kill as many of Ant's men as it took for me to get to him. Right now though, my focus had to be on making sure the rest of my family was safe. I called Bridgette first, and she answered on the second ring.

"N-Nate, th-they shot..."

"I know. I saw. Where are you?" I asked, tasting the bitter beginnings of grief on my tongue.

"I don't-I don't know where I am. I was right around the corner from Mom's house when the video went live, and I-I just kept driving. I think I'm in Old Town Alexandria right now."

"Is Yah Yah with you?" I asked, hopeful.

"No, but she texted and said that she's safe. She said that she was gonna keep running until you or I guaranteed her safety."

"Okay, that's good. That's smart, but you gotta tell her to get out of Virginia asap. We don't need to know where she's headed right now, but it can't be anywhere in Virginia. Okay?" I asked.

"I'll tell her. What about you though? Where will you go?"

The response on the tip of my tongue was that I was going to hell, and I was happily taking Ant with me, but I wasn't ready to self-destruct. At least not yet anyway.

"I'm gonna get my wife and son to safety," I replied.

"Nathan, please. I know-I know that someone killing our mother is unforgivable, but I beg you not to go out there and get yourself killed too."

"Sis, you know that I'm smarter than that... But the person responsible *will* answer for what they've done, and I put that on God. Call me when you're out of the state and don't stop driving until you've at least made it that far," I said, hanging up before she could offer any more protests about my next moves.

Even in my wife's concentrated silence, I could feel her desire to give the same speech that my sister had attempted. It was not because she'd actually given her thoughts away through any type of physical cue, but my wife was my best friend, and I knew her better than she knew herself. Just like I knew that she would, she fought her temptation by focusing on getting to our son as soon as possible. While she drove in silence, I started sending messages as fast as I could, calling in ever favor owed to me because I wanted every shooter on the open market gunning for Ant. While I was in the middle of doing that, I got a message from my brother, Stuckey, saying that he'd be in Virginia by nightfall, and he was bringing some friends with him. Stuckey was birthed in the mud and raised in the streets, but since we had the same pops and different moms, he didn't grow up with Bridgette, me, or Yah Yah. Still, we were close, and I knew that he loved my mother just as much as he did his own, which meant that he'd ride into this storm with me without hesitation. I let him know that I was in the process of making sure Tay and Peanut got out of harm's way, and then I'd meet him at the safehouse in D.C. My brother and I thought the same way, which was why I'd helped him pick out and finish his safehouse in D.C. just like he'd done mine in Maryland. Despite the fact that I'd worked and played in Virginia, I knew that if I ever had to burn some bridges then I needed a spot to hold up in outside of the Commonwealth.

"Baby, we're almost there. How are we gonna do this?" Tay asked, looking over at me.

The daycare center that our son attended was like a private school for toddlers and babies, but it was worth every penny.

The biggest selling point for us had been how they went overboard on security, and moments like this made it worth it.

"You go in and get him, baby, and I'll hold shit down out here. Be quick."

She nodded in understanding, and a few minutes later, we pulled up in front of the school. I waited until she hopped out before I chambered a round in the pistol now in my grip, and then my eyes were roaming like a spotlight in a prison yard. It was ten long minutes before my wife and son emerged from the building. I could see my little man's mouth moving a mile a minute as he talked his mom's ear off the way only a two-year-old could. I tucked the pistol and got out to open the back door for her to put him in his car seat. As soon as he saw me, his arms shot out for me to take him, and I could feel the instant smile that he always put on my face. I took him and covered his tiny face with kisses as I put him in his seat and strapped him in. I made sure to give him his tablet before shutting the door so that he would be occupied, and then I got back in the passenger seat.

"Are we going back home?" Tay asked, looking over at me.

Part of me wanted to believe that my home was still safe, but in my mind's eye, I kept seeing my mother getting shot in the head. I refused to gamble with my wife and son.

"Nah, head to the beach house in Ocean City," I replied.

My decision to head deeper into Maryland was based on the fact that neither me nor anyone in my family had any ties to the beach house that I owned. It was a gift that had been given years ago by a business associate, and I'd turned it into a beautiful fortress. There were definitely worse places to hide out. As she got back on the road, I went back to my phone and continued to move pieces on the chess board until I was satisfied that I wasn't playing from a position of being on my heels. It took us a little more than forty-five minutes to make it to the beach house, and then, it was another half an hour before we were settled inside.

"I'm gonna change Peanut and fix something to eat. Do you want anything, boo?" she asked.

"Nah, I'm good."

I could feel her desire to say more because that was the nurturer in her, and I loved her for it, but right now, I felt like I needed to feel all the pain in my heart. When our eyes locked, I saw the question in hers, which made me cross the room and kiss her gently on the forehead.

"I love you, Nathan, and I know that this is gonna change you, but don't let it destroy the amazing man that you've become."

"I won't, babe," I vowed softly.

She took a tiny step back while looking up at me and sticking her left pinky finger out toward me. I couldn't help smiling because she was the only person in the world who could make my grown ass pinky promise like we were both still kids. I loved how she tapped into my innocence because that was where my humanity resided. I knew that I would need constant reminding of that humanity in the days to come because I was fighting monsters and demons from the inside out. After our pinkies locked, she sealed the deal with a quick kiss, and then she left me standing in the middle of the bedroom we shared. I didn't know exactly what my next move should be, so I stripped off all of my clothes and headed into the bathroom to take a hot shower. I was secretly hoping that the heat of the water and the pounding pressure of the spray would ease some of the anxiety in my body, but once I was trapped inside the shower's steam, my subconscious spoke up. Without warning, more tears began to pour from my eyes and blur my vision, but I didn't try to run from them or the despair that they represented. Because of everything that I'd been through in my life in terms of heartbreaks, misplaced trust, and prison, I kept a tight hold on my emotions at all times. It felt good to finally let go though, and when I did, I could feel the relief entwined with the sadness as my tears rained faster than the showerhead over top of me. I didn't know how long I spent in my private cocoon of grief, but I felt more focused and capable when I stepped out of the shower. I went in search of a towel, and once I dried off, I grabbed a pair of stonewashed jeans and a plain white t-shirt to put on. After I was dressed, I wandered up the hallway to the kitchen where I found my two favorite people eating sandwiches.

"Where's mine at?" I asked.

"I figured that you'd want something else to snack on," she replied, pushing a big ass cookie in my direction.

I immediately recognized that this wasn't an ordinary cookie. It was one cooked with pure love and high amounts of THC. When I gave her a quizzical look, she didn't blink or flinch.

"You need to take the edge off, and you know that we don't keep anything to smoke here unless it's a planned staycation. You're stressed the fuck out though, bae, and I get it, so just try to relax a little," she said gently.

I nodded in thanks and agreement as I picked up the cookie and bit it. Of course, as soon as Peanut saw me eating something sweet, he was no longer interested in his turkey and cheese sandwich, and he began to whine while reaching toward me.

"Stop being fat and spoiled, boy," I said, chuckling as I moved to get him a few regular chocolate chip cookies.

"You *know* that he's spoiled, Nate, and it's all your fault."

The look that I gave her over my shoulder let her know that I was calling bullshit, and she started laughing instantly. In the midst of her laughing, her phone started pinging again, which had me patting my pockets for my own, and that was when I realized that I'd left it on the bed next to the pistol. I continued on my mission of getting my son his cookies, but my mind wasn't here in this house right now.

"Is someone messaging you?" I asked, giving Peanut his cookies and focusing on her face that was buried in her phone.

"It's-it's another Instagram Live video."

Without waiting for an explanation, I plucked the phone from her fingers and checked for myself. The first thing that I saw was a face that was as familiar as it was foreign, and it put the putrid taste of fresh hate on my tongue where grief had not long ago resided. I mentally prepared myself to the best of my ability, and then I accessed the video.

"As most of you know, tonight is my annual Breast Cancer Awareness banquet held in our nation's capital in honor of all breast cancer survivors and in remembrance of those lost to that courageous battle. Although I did not personally know Marcela Ty, I'm told that she was such a brave and courageous woman who was battling cancer before she was senselessly gunned down a little while ago today. While I'm sure that her family is mourning and rightfully so, I invite one and all to come out to my banquet tonight in celebration of Marcela Ty. Any and all donations made tonight will be divided equally between my nonprofit organization and the Ty family. I understand that no amount of money will make up for the tragedy of such senseless violence, but it's important that we as a people stand with her and her family. I know the pain of loss... intimately... And I offer my condolences to the Ty family. For more details about the banquet or to find out how to make donations, please visit my official website..."

"Baby, are you-are you okay?" Tay asked.

I could feel the shaking reverberating throughout my body even before I saw the shaking in my hand, and I knew that my control was rapidly evaporating.

"I'm gonna kill 'em."

"Kill who, baby? The guy throwing the banquet? Boo, he's just trying to help and..."

"He's *not* trying to help!" I exploded angrily.

My tone caused her to jump, and Peanut's cookies were instantly forgotten because he immediately started crying. Both reactions were like ice water being thrown on the fast-growing fire inside me, and I was granted a reprieve from the inferno that wanted to engulf me.

"That man, the one who made the sincere sounding video, isn't trying to do anything except twist the knife that's already in my heart," I said.

"What do you mean, baby? Why would he do that?"

"Because that man is responsible for my mother's death. That man is Ant," I said softly.

6

"Wait, so-so you're saying that the muthafucka in that video is responsible for what happened to Mom? I don't understand. Nate, why would he get on Instagram and give that speech? Why dedicate his banquet to a woman whose murder he orchestrated?"

"Because he's playing in my face. He's intentionally provoking me to do some shit that I can't get away with by making himself look like a good guy and the bigger person."

"I don't understand though because it won't be hard for someone to put the pieces together about the two niggas you hit this morning being related to him, and that makes him an automatic suspect for what happened to Mom," she said.

"That nigga is too arrogant to give a fuck, and right now, he's playing offense in order to make the police and public doubt his involvement in my mom's killing. I know what he did though, and I don't give a fuck how many banquets he throws because I'm gonna bury that nigga," I said, pulling my t-shirt off over my head as I headed back into the bathroom.

I dropped the shirt, took off my jeans, and then headed into the walk-in closet where we kept outfits for every occasion. I picked out a black, two-piece, Black Billionaire suit, matching black, silk, button up shirt, gray Tom Ford tie, and a pair of gray Gucci loafers. When I emerged from the closet and laid the clothes on the bed, I came face-to-face with my wife. Her cheeks were still glistening from the recently shed tears, but she appeared to have the crying under control for the moment. My first thought was that she'd achieved the goal of control thanks to the sniffer of amber alcohol in her left hand, but the determination swimming in her river of tears said something different.

"Baby, I know that you gotta do this, so I'm not gonna try to talk you out of it. I am gonna beg you to think this through though. If you go at this nigga with your raw emotions exposed, he's gonna run circles around you and then kill you on Instagram just because. I don't want the memory of your execution to be what I or your son internalizes because that will eat us alive. Which means I'll be watching the two men that I love the most die over and over again. I need you to use all of your mental prowess to beat this muthafucka and come back home to us. Do you understand?" she asked, passing me the glass of liquor.

I took it and swallowed half of the Henny in one gulp without taking my eyes off of her beauty. I was consciously memorizing every line, blemish, and crease in her face because I knew that I'd need these memories once I let the darkness completely consume me. She was my light, and she'd been that from the day she gave herself over to our love. I knew that her and Peanut were the best parts of me, but I was gonna have to shut them out and embrace the monster that I kept hidden in the shadows. I quickly finished my drink, set the glass on the nightstand, and then pulled my wife into my arms.

"I love you, Shytavia Lakia, and I need you to remember that no matter how this plays out."

"Show me," she whispered, linking her arms around my neck.

Without hesitation, my lips descended on hers with a possessive hunger that made her pulse quicken as her heart beat faster against my chest. My passion and hunger for her were high on a normal day, but the reality of this possibly being our last time making love had me filled with unspeakable desperation. I pulled her t-shirt over her head, and then I pushed her leggings down to her ankles so that she could step out of them. While I was doing that, she released the barrette that was holding her braids back, and suddenly, her fifty-eight-inch plats were tumbling sexily around her shoulders and titties.

"You're so beautiful," I said in a husky tone.

"You're biased, boo, but thank you," she replied, blushing and smiling.

I grabbed two fistfuls of her hair and pulled her mouth back to mine, branding her with the heat of my lips and tongue so that she'd never forget who she belonged to. Once I knew that she was sufficiently drunk off of my kisses, I spun her around and pulled her back against my chest fast enough to make her gasp. My left hand grabbed her braids and wrapped them around my knuckles as I lowered my lips to her right shoulder and kissed my way to her neck. With deliberate, slow force, I turned her head to the left, licked slowly up her neck to her jaw line, and then I bit her gently along the same path. The way that her body shuddered was so thrilling that my dick instantly got harder. I pushed my boxers down to my feet and kicked them off while bending her over enough for me to push my throbbing dick beyond the protective barrier of her thick pussy lips. The moment that the tip of my dick was introduced to her hot honey, I took a steadying breath and kept pushing until I was buried inside her earth like one who'd been called home to glory. My mind told me to take a moment and adjust, but I ignored that by pulling out of her fast and diving back inside of her soaking wet pussy harder. She threw that ass back at me, but I bent her all the way over the bed and drilled her like construction work put food on the table. I could feel her whole body vibrating, almost like it was singing to me, and I knew that melody intimately. My grip on her hair got tighter as my other hand went to her hip, and I was trying to break her back. I fucked her like it was the first time and the last time, and once I felt her cum on my dick twice, I allowed myself to join her and willfully drown in her volcanic ocean. Only once my cum stopped shooting inside her did I let her hair go and allow her to collapse face first on the bed.

"You okay?" I asked, chuckling as I laid down beside her and pulled her into my arms.

"You're an asshole for that," she said, punching me lightly in the shoulder as she settled into my embrace.

"You knew that I was an asshole when you met me, Tay, and you married me anyway."

"You're right, and you knew that I was crazy, so what's your point?" she asked, grabbing my dick while looking up at me.

"My point is that I love you, baby... for real."

I hadn't meant to make the moment a heavy one, but she was staring at me now with her whole heart in her eyes. She'd never been more beautiful, and Lord knows that I didn't want to lose her, but whatever my destiny was had already been written before this moment.

"I love you too, baby, and that's why you gotta promise to come back to me and our son," she replied.

"I gotchu, sweetheart."

"That ain't enough this time, Nathan. I need you to promise me," she insisted, holding her hand out.

"I pinky promise, my love. I'll come back to you and our son," I vowed, locking fingers with her and kissing her softly.

She responded with the same tenderness, but within seconds, I could taste the salt of her tears mixed in with our kisses. She abruptly pulled away from me, hopped up, and headed to the bathroom. I laid there, aching to go to her but knowing that offering her lies wasn't fair to either of us. I took a deep breath before getting up and getting dressed, and then, I went to check on my little man because he was too quiet. I found him at the table with his little head slumped on his chest, snoring lightly, and all I could do was smile. I stood there and watched him for a few seconds more, and then, I picked him up gently so that I could go lay him down for his nap. Once I had him in his bed, I grabbed my phone and headed outside to the back deck so that I could put my plans for tonight in motion. I was a lot of things, but one thing that I knew for sure was that this nigga, Ant, was gonna learn real quick that I was too stupid to run from him. The first thing that I did was let my brother, Stuckey, know that we were attending a black-tie event at the Trump Hotel in D.C. I asked him if he needed me to get him a date since this was a last-minute thing, and that got me cussed out with a reminder that he was the one who gave me 'the game'. I apologized for my disrespect and then texted the woman who I intended to be my date for the night while heading back inside.

"Why do you got that evil ass smile on your face?" Tay asked, wrapping a towel around her body.

"Because my little brother thinks that he got all the sense."

"Oh, Lawd, you two are the most competitive muthafuckas I've ever met. Do I even wanna know what this is about?" she asked.

"Nah, not for real."

I didn't look at her when I replied, but I could feel her eyes burning a nice sized hole through the frontal lobe of my brain. I kept my focus on the texts that I was exchanging though because I was meeting resistance to my request for a dinner companion. I hated to be pushy, but I wasted no time reminding the female that she owed me several times over. Within a couple minutes, she agreed to make me her plus one, and that allowed me to turn my attention back to my wife.

"I got a few hours before the event, so I'mma head to the city and be ready for Stuckey to arrive," I said.

"Baby, are you sure that this is such a good idea? I mean, you're going to a highly visible event, inside the swamp that is D.C. politics, after you were just seen executing two kids a few hours ago."

" I'm sure that I'll be the topic of conversation, but I can promise you that no one is expecting me to be there," I replied, smirking.

"Well, that's for damn sure."

"Right, and when people get caught off guard, they tend to make mistakes because you're catching them without their mask on," I stated confidently.

She nodded, but I couldn't tell if it was in agreement or resignation that she couldn't change my mind. She crossed the distance between us, stood on her tippy toes, and kissed me gently.

"Hurry back to us," she whispered.

Before I could respond, she'd turned and left the room without a backwards glance. I wanted to go to her and make love to her until all she felt was safety and the warmth of my heart beating beneath her touch. I knew that the only way to make that our reality again was to stay the course of action I'd set into motion. I took a deep breath as I refocused on the night ahead. I called and ordered a car using one of my clean aliases, and half an hour later, I was in the back of a navy-blue Lincoln Town Car. When I got to my brother's safe house, I let myself in since my DNA and fingerprints were a part of his security system. Once I was behind closed doors, I immediately began to pull out weapons that we'd need, along with closed circuit earpieces, and then I contacted my 'date' for the night. I arranged to pick her up within the next couple hours, and then my mission was studying the digital blueprints of the hotel where the banquet was being held. Security would undoubtedly be impenetrable, so trying to walk in there with a gun wasn't my move.

Especially given the fact that I was gonna be on everyone's radar all night long. Despite my desire to dump bullets into Ant's face, I knew that this required intelligence, finesse, and more than a little patience. My ultimate goal was to negotiate an agreement of peace that I had no intention of keeping because sometimes retreating was the first offensive move. My approach was sure to confuse Ant as much as my presence at the event he'd dedicated to the woman he'd murdered. I concealed two eight-inch ceramic knives on me, and then, I picked out matching Glock .27s for Stuckey. I knew that his credentials in security would allow him to attend the event with almost any type of weapon on him, but I chose the Glocks because I knew how much he loved them. After that, I picked him out a tux to wear and some matching Tom Ford loafers, which meant that all he had to do was get ready once he arrived. When I went to text him to find out exactly when he'd be pulling up, I found a message from Marissa, my date, telling me to get to her house asap because we needed to talk before the event. I should've anticipated this because I could tell by her tone earlier that she'd had no idea what type of day I'd had. Her message now read differently. I sent a message to Stuckey, telling him that I'd meet him at the banquet because I had to pick up my date, and then I went back outside to the waiting car. I gave the driver Marissa's address in Northwest D.C., and then I sat back for the ride. It had been almost a year since I'd seen Marissa in person, but her 5'4", one hundred forty pounds hadn't changed since she was a sixteen-year-old lifeguard at my neighborhood pool. Most white girls feared Washington D.C. when I was growing up because it was a city that stole souls, but Marissa hadn't been afraid because she grew up right next door in Arlington, Virginia. She was beautiful with natural red hair, and she was as crazy as the day was long on any plantation. Within twenty minutes, I'd arrived at her house, and I stepped out of my memories into the present while making sure to adjust my instincts to tune into the environment around me. By the time I made it up the sidewalk to her front steps, she was standing in her doorway. She looked breathtaking in a form fitting black dress with fire in her green eyes.

"When you demanded to be my plus one to tonight's banquet. you left out some important information, Nathan."

"Like what?" I asked, feigning innocence —_or ignorance at the very least.

"Well, let's start with the fact that I am the chief of police, and you just got away with *two* coldblooded murders, you son of a bitch!"

7

"You might wanna watch your tone," I said, moving past her into the house.

"I didn't invite you in, and my family is upstairs sleeping."

"Then I suggest you fix your tone when you're talking to me and let's take this conversation to your home office," I suggested, continuing to walk through her house like I owned it.

I heard the door close behind us and then the sound of her heels rhythmically clicking on the faux marble floor as she followed me around the corner and down the hall. When I came to her office, I opened the door and waited for her to walk through it before I followed and shut the door to any prying eyes or perky ears.

"Why didn't you tell me what happened, Nate?"

"I honestly thought that you would've heard about it already, especially given the fact that it was filmed on

Instagram Live," I replied, taking a seat on the corner of her desk.

"I'm too busy trying to keep this city safe to be on social media all day long, and you know that."

"So, I take it that Ava hasn't seen it either because she would've come to you immediately," I said, feeling a small sense of relief.

"Ordinarily, I'd say you're right, but Ava's been acting differently with me lately."

"Different how?" I asked, concerned.

"She's nineteen, Nate, and I'm sure that you remember what type of rebellion comes with that age. We can talk about that later though because, right now, you need to tell me what the fuck is going on, and you better not *think* about lying," she replied, standing right in front of me and crossing her arms over her big titties.

My mind flashed back to many times when we were younger and the same fiery temperament had been brought to the surface by something I'd done. As inappropriate as it was in this moment, I couldn't help the laughter that bubbled up and escaped between my lips.

"I'm glad that I amuse you, but I'm not laughing, Nathan, and I'm not going *anywhere* with you until you tell me what the fuck you're asking me to step into."

"Calm down, damn. I'll tell you everything, and you already know that because we keep secrets together, not *from* each other. You're still cute when you're mad though."

"Flirt with your wife because I'm not buying what you're selling. Start talking," she demanded.

I kept my smartass comments to myself and explained

what happened from the time I arrived at my mother's house this morning. By the time I'd finished running shit down, Marissa had poured both of us a glass of tequila, and she was sipping from hers while staring at me over the rim of the glass.

"I always said that you knew how to dig a grave," she said, shaking her head.

"Are you really about to stand there and say that this shit is my fault, Marissa?"

"No, because not all of it is, but I doubt that you're ready to face the real culprit," she replied.

"Of course I am. Why do you think that I'm going to the banquet?"

"I'm not talking about Ant. I'm talking about your sister, Yah Yah. You know like I do that she set you up and..."

"Don't go there," I warned, tossing back the shot of tequila and sitting the glass on her desk as I stood up.

For a moment, she stared at me with an amused smirk on her face, but she eventually raised her hands to signal the end to that line of inquiry.

"Okay, Nate, so we're gonna go to this event to prove what exactly?"

"We're just going to ruffle some feathers and see what shakes loose."

"I'm not buying the innocence in your tone, plus I've known you too well to believe that you're actually letting this go," she said seriously.

"You're right, and of course I'm not letting it go, but I'm also not putting you in harm's way. So, tonight is just about shock value. Don't worry. Stuckey is coming too."

"I thought that your brother was in Atlanta. When did he come back?" she asked.

"He just got here, and I called for him to come up here after shit went bad this morning. Don't worry. He's gonna play nice for now."

"Nate, I've known your brother almost as long as I've known you, and *nice* isn't something that he does well. That was before he joined the CIA."

"I think that joining the CIA calmed him down somewhat."

"No, it gave him a license to kill whoever needed killing, which allowed him to better hide his true nature and stay off of anyone's radar."

"I guess it's a shame that they didn't recruit both of us for their wet work," I replied, smirking.

She opened her mouth to say something, but the sound of her office door opening caught both of our attention and made her turn around.

"I thought that I heard your voice," Ava said.

"Sweetie, when did you get home?" Marissa asked.

"Just now," Ava replied, still not taking her eyes off of me.

"Is everything alright, Ava?" Marissa asked.

"I don't know. Why don't you two tell me? How is a man that killed two people less than twelve hours ago standing beside you, obviously free, looking casket sharp to match your own evening wear, Mother?"

"Sweetie, it's a long story, and I..."

"Of course it's a long story, Mom, because it involves him, but it's not *your* story, so why don't you let him tell it for once?" Ava said with barely controlled anger lacing her words.

"Marissa, give us a minute," I said softly.

She looked back at me with fear in her eyes, but I gave her a smile that I knew she'd trust because she was one of the few people who knew my soul.

"I'll meet you in the car," she said, turning and heading for the door.

Once she closed the door behind her, I took a deep breath and tried to gauge exactly how mad Ava was.

"What's on your mind, sweetheart?"

"Oh, I don't know. I'm just trying to understand how someone so smart could be dumb enough to shoot two niggas on Instagram," she replied sarcastically.

"I was set up, and that should be obvious to someone with your intellect. So, why don't you tell me why you're really mad, Ava?"

"Because you're my dad, and someone is either targeting you for death or prison, but in either scenario, I'm not ready to lose you," she replied, choking up as her anger gave way to pain.

When I held my arms open, she quickly crossed the room and clung to me, and seconds later, I could feel the heat of her tears on my neck.

"Shhh, sweetheart, it's all gonna be okay. I promise. You're not getting rid of me that easily."

"But Dad, I..."

"No buts, Ava. I just need you to trust me the same way that you always have. You know that I've got more lives than ten alley cats, and I'm a hard man to beat on my worst day. Today was a bad day, but it wasn't my worst."

"What about what happened to Grandma though?" she asked, pulling back and looking up at me.

Part of me had secretly been hoping that my baby girl hadn't witnessed her grandmother's execution, but social media was her generations' lifeline, so they couldn't function without it. Ava was a secret to almost everyone in my life because her mom and I had agreed to keep her out of harm's way by not letting it be known that I was her dad. My mom had been one of the select people who knew, and Ava had had a relationship with her grandma from the time she was a baby. As much as losing my mom hurt me, I knew that it was crushing my daughter, and that made me pull her back to me.

"Your grandma's not in pain anymore, and she would want you to focus on that, sweetheart."

I felt more tears on my skin as she nodded and continued to cry softly. I knew that I couldn't take her pain away, and I couldn't make her understand, so I simply held my daughter and pushed back against the helplessness trying to consume me. Once she was cried out for the moment, she took a step backwards out of my arms and wiped her face with the palms of her hands.

"Where are you and Mom going?"

"To a banquet that's honoring your grandmother," I replied neutrally.

"I wanna go so that I can pay my respects."

"I understand, but it's not a good idea for you to be in the same room as me right now, especially when we know I'm a target," I reasoned.

"It's not any safer for Mom to be with you either," she argued.

"Your mom is the chief of police for all of Washington D.C., so odds are that I'm safer with her than the occupants of the White House. Besides, tonight is about business. You'll get to pay your respects when we have her funeral. For now, I just need you to lay low and stay close to the house when you're not on campus."

"I'm taking some time off from school, Dad. I told Mom that I wanted to be the one to tell you, but that's a conversation that we can have later. Go do what you gotta do," she said.

"Where's your phone?" I asked, pulling mine out of my pocket and scrolling through my photo gallery.

When she pulled hers out, I tapped my phone against hers, and all the pictures of her brother, Peanut, that I'd tagged were sent to her device.

"He's getting bigger and badder," I said, kissing her briefly on the forehead.

"Sounds just like you. By the way, when exactly are you planning to tell your wife about me?"

"You know that's up to your mom, sweetheart. I can't make her trust Tay, but maybe she needs to hear from you that you're ready to meet my wife and your baby brother. Talk to her," I advised.

The way Ava rolled her eyes reminded me of her mom at that age, causing me to laugh softly as I walked out of the room. I found Marissa sitting patiently in the back of my rented car with her attention on her phone when I climbed in beside her.

"I already gave him the address," she informed me right before we pulled off.

My phone buzzed, and when I looked at it, I saw a message from my brother.

"Stuckey is on his way too."

"How's Ava?" she asked.

"She's scared, but you know how tough she is. She'll be okay."

"She'll be okay as long as you stay alive, Nate, so you better do everything in your power to stay that way," she said, reaching out and taking my hand.

When I looked over at her, I saw the genuine concern in the shifting of her eye color that glowed jade green in the moonlight, and it was reminiscent of the look I'd just seen in our daughter's ash gray eyes. Promises to never die were lies that both the giver and receiver recognized upon delivery, but still the words were uttered and accepted. I had no intentions of dying anytime in the near future, but my gut told me that I was gonna have to kill a lot more people to escape death's grip this time. No one could run forever, and by all accounts, I'd had a helluva run.

"Ava is pressing the issue about meeting Shytavia and Asaiah," I said, changing the subject.

"Do you think that she's ready?"

"She hasn't been a baby for a long time now, so yeah, I think that she can handle it," I replied.

"I wasn't talking about Ava. I was talking about your wife. This is a big secret that you've been keeping, Nate, and no matter what pretty words you use, it's still gonna affect your marriage."

"If I didn't know any better, I'd suspect that this was your intent," I said.

"But you do know better, and you know that my interest is only ever to keep our daughter safe. I've never once wanted to deny you your happiness."

Part of me wanted to deny the truth of her words, but that didn't make sense, so I just left it alone, and we rode in silence. When we arrived at the banquet hall, there were reporters and paparazzi like this was billed to be a star-studded event, which wasn't the case as far as I knew.

"A lot of cameras," I mumbled.

"Yeah, and a lot of publicity makes getting away with murder unlikely, even for your lucky ass. So, don't do anything stupid," she whispered back. "Take us to the side entrance. Some of my men should be there," she instructed the driver.

"What's wrong, sweetheart? You don't want our picture on the front page of the Washington Post?"

"Exactly," she replied, ducking down in the seat as we drove past the front entrance.

When we came to a stop in the alley, four men stepped out and opened the back doors for us, and we were quickly ushered inside.

"I need to work the room real quick and lay down my cover story about personally knowing your mom before you and I are spotted together. Can I trust you to stay out of trouble?" she asked.

"Of course you can. I..."

"Well, well, if it isn't Nathan Ty, aka Nate Dawg. I'm surprised to see you here and in the company of the chief of police no less."

I turned to the sound of his voice coming from my

right, and I knew the face that I would find as if I'd seen it in the mirror every morning I'd awakened.

"What's up, Ant? Long time no see."

8

"I was sorry to hear about your mom, Nate. It's just tragic and senseless," Ant said.

"That it was. That it was. When God calls you home to glory though, we don't have any choice in the matter. The same goes for the devil I suppose," I replied, keeping my tone even despite the hatred seething within me.

When our eyes locked, I could see the glint of madness burning brightly within his iris, and there was no sense of reason in sight. The Ant that I remembered had at least a foothold on reality, but the man standing before me in the tailor-made suit was someone different. I took an unflinching step toward him to show him that I towered over his six-foot height, and I outweighed his two hundred pounds. I made sure that my gaze stayed locked with his so that he could see that there was absolutely no fear in me, and I made sure that I was close enough for him to hear me.

"Death comes for us all, Anthony, and I'm bringing yours," I whispered.

"A hollow threat at best but then again, you always did think you were the smartest slave on the plantation," he replied, smiling broadly.

I felt Marissa pulling on my arm at the exact same time I caught movement in my peripheral vision. Before her face came fully into view, I knew who the woman moving to stand beside Ant was. In reality, she was what caused the madness to still burn inside of this man now, but he wouldn't admit to being whooped by some pussy that was mediocre at best. Her mama had named her Diamond, but in the streets, she was known as Pretty Girl, and the nickname was well deserved. She looked like Pocahontas with her tanned, sun kissed skin, and her body was damn near flawless when it came to her thick thighs, tiny waist, plump ass, and firm titties. All of this was currently concealed by the stunning, black, off the shoulder, floor length Black Billionaire dress molded to her, but I knew her body well enough to remember what lied beneath. She stood only 5'2", but the six-inch heels she was wearing gave her an Amazon quality that only enhanced her beauty.

"Pretty Girl... I see that you're still slumming," I said, smirking at Ant.

I could feel Marissa squeezing my bicep, and it kept me in check for the moment.

"Nathan, I'm surprised to see you here... and with the police chief," Pretty Girl said.

Before this moment, I'd harbored no ill feelings toward her because I was just as responsible as she was for our complicated past, but her being here with him signaled a new era in our relationship. There was no doubt in my mind that she knew her man was responsible for my mother's death, and yet she was still standing beside him. To me that meant that she had that same blood on her hands too.

"Come on, Nate. Not here," Marissa whispered, pulling on my arm gently.

Feeling the rage surging through me, I didn't resist her pull this time, and I resigned myself to being patient. Revenge was best served cold for a reason.

"Enjoy the party, Nate. Your mom would be proud of the big turnout for her send off," Ant said.

I could feel the ripples of maliciousness race up my spine, but I kept moving away from them both in order to maintain my sanity.

"Breathe, Nate," Marissa said, looping her arm through mine and escorting me to a quiet corner.

When the first waiter passed, I grabbed a glass of champagne and guzzled it in its entirety.

"Don't get drunk. It'll only make it worse," Marissa admonished.

"I'm not trying to get drunk. I'm just trying to settle my nerves before I go on a massive killing spree in this bitch."

"I need you to remember that this was your idea, despite my very vocal protests, and for that reason, you *will* keep your killing to a bare minimum. If that ain't enough of a reason then I need you to remember that I was the last person our daughter saw you with, which means that she's gonna blame me for whatever happens. Don't put me in that position," she said.

Her words caused me to look over at her, and that kinda gave me a reality check to stop the roaring blood rushing through my veins that demanded me to kill 'em all. The last thing that I needed was to cause friction between my daughter and her mom because I knew how close they were. Marissa had two other younger children by her new husband, but her relationship with Ava was different because they'd basically grown up together. Ava had pushed Marissa into adulthood and kept her there, so I knew that one layer of their relationship was gratitude from mother to daughter. I respected that.

"Don't worry. I'm gonna keep it together until it's time to act a damn fool," I said, smiling mischievously.

"Good. Now, I'm going to make my rounds so play nice."

We shared a moment of pause where I could feel her reluctance to let go of my arm, but I gave her a reassuring nod, and she moved off into the crowd. My eyes scanned the room, impressed by the turnout despite the evil intent of the host. The people who'd come didn't know the back story. They were just here for a worthy cause, and I respected that. The feeling of my phone vibrating in my pocket pulled my attention away from the crowd as I pulled it out and checked my text messages. My brother's message was alerting me of his arrival, and I looked up toward the entrance of the quickly filling ballroom. The anticipation I felt at seeing Stuckey brought about a feeling of relief, but it was swiftly crushed by the sight of my ex approaching me.

"I'm not in the mood, Diamond."

"Those are words that I've never heard you say to me before," she replied, smirking as she snatched a glass of champagne from a passing waiter and drinking some.

"You're hearing them now. I'd advise you to go back to Ant before I lose my temper."

"Oooh, not you threatening to lose your temper with little ole me," she said with heavy sarcasm.

"Diamond, you better play where it's safe," I stated in a deadly tone.

The mischievous fun that had been dancing in her eyes evaporated as she took a step closer to me, seemingly so that we wouldn't be overheard.

"I didn't know about your mom, Nate. I would never do that to you... or to me. I may not know you as well as your wife does, but I know that you intend to kill everyone connected to Ant. Yes, I'm in a very complicated relationship with him, but I need you to spare me."

"Spare you? And what the fuck makes you think that I would do that?" I asked, feeling my anger rising like a summer temperature.

My question caused her to stare at me for several moments before she drained the rest of her champagne and handed her empty glass off to a waiter.

"I would think that you could spare me because of our history together, but I can tell by the look on your face that I shouldn't bet my life on that. How about this for a reason?" she asked, digging in her clutch purse and coming out with her phone.

I felt my patience growing thinner than mint Girl Scout cookies, but I kept my cool because I caught sight of Stuckey passing through customs to enter the ballroom over Diamond's right shoulder. Time was running out for everyone in the room.

"You don't want your man to see you talking to me, so I'd advise you to hurry up and get out my face."

She glared at me for a second, and then she turned her

phone toward me. The picture of the girl on the screen looked like a mirror image of the woman standing before me, just younger... and there was something about her eyes. When I looked back up at Pretty Girl, I suddenly saw all of her years melt away and transport us back to a different time and place. It was a time before Ant became all-knowing and all seeing like the great and powerful wizard of Oz.

"Who is she?" I asked softly.

Before Pretty Girl could answer, Ant appeared behind her with the swiftness of a vampire, and suddenly, my attention was back on the moment at hand.

"This is a private conversation, Anthony," I said, becoming the necessary distraction that allowed her to slip her phone back inside of her clutch.

"I see that, but I'm wondering what the fuck you two could possibly be discussing of such importance," he replied, grabbing her elbow possessively.

"I-I just wanted him to leave because I knew that he was only here to provoke you," she said, taking a step backwards so that she was leaning up against Ant's chest.

"By all means, let him stay. All of this is for him anyway," Ant said, leading her away from me and merging with the crowd.

I took a few seconds to regain my composure, and by that time, Stuckey had crossed the room to me.

"Damn, bruh," he said, opening his arms and giving me a heartfelt hug.

"Thanks for coming, bruh."

"You would never have to ask twice. Do you want me to just shoot the nigga now?" he asked.

His question made me smile because I'd known that he'd waste no time swimming into the deep waters with me.

"Patience, bruh. We need to see how many people are with this nigga so that we don't get hit with a well-placed shot to the back of the head."

"I hear you. I've got four people with me," he replied.

"Okay. I've got Marissa with me, and she's praying that we can do this without all hell breaking loose."

"I feel her on that, but it all depends on how willing Ant is to go into that gentle night. We're somewhat covered as long as we can make the killing look provoked on his part because I talked to my handler about Ant. He's already been considered an enemy of the state. Nobody will miss him when he's gone, and I'll probably get a nice bonus," he said, smiling.

"Well, if all we need to do is provoke him, then I know just what button to push," I replied, giving my brother a knowing look.

He chuckled softly in understanding.

"Let's spread out and evaluate the situation. Put your earpiece in."

I nodded before heading in the opposite direction of Stuckey and discreetly moving the small mic to my ear. As I was making my way around the room, I noticed the huge picture that Ant had blown up and put on an easel at the front of the ballroom. I could feel my heart in my throat as both sadness and fury warred inside of me. This nigga, Ant, was most definitely playing in my face, and I could feel the hatred magnifying by the second, but I remained focused. There were several armed men moving through the crowd with visible earpieces in their ears, signaling that they were the hired help, but I was looking for the less visible ops.

"I've spotted six hired guns," I murmured softly.

"Yeah, I peeped them too, but they're the distraction. It's a couple niggas in here that look way too uncomfortable in tuxedos to be anything other than active street niggas," Stuckey replied.

His assessment had me looking at the guests differently, and I immediately saw what he meant. I spotted three of them, but the fact that they were headed out of the front door of the banquet hall confused me.

"Can you look more obvious?" Marissa asked, sliding up next to me and looping her arm through mine.

"What are you talking about?" I asked defensively.

"Nate, only a blind man wouldn't know that you're scoping out the room on demon time," she replied, giving me a fake smile.

I could hear Stuckey snickering in my ear, which only added to the frustration that I was feeling because of her chastising me.

"Stuckey, shut the fuck up or I'mma shoot you in your leg like I did when we were fifteen," I threatened.

"As I recall, you doing that got you shot in the right ass cheek as payback, and I got stuck with the job of changing your bandages. I *won't* be doing that again, so if you fuck around, you're gonna be ass out," she said.

Again, I could hear my brother laughing in my ear, and the memory of that summer that I spent sleeping on my stomach flashed back into my mind. It quickly vanished though when Marissa and I were approached by an unexpected guest.

"What the fuck are you doing here?" I asked immediately.

"Dad, chill, I just didn't feel right sitting out on such an important event for Grandma. Besides, I'm safe with you two," Ava replied.

"Ava, you need to go home now," Marissa said, taking a step toward her.

"Bruh, we've got movement at the front," Stuckey announced.

When my eyes skated in that direction, I caught sight of one of the hired security slipping out the front door to the banquet hall, just like Ant's goons had. I quickly scanned the crowd, looking for the rest of the security, but I didn't see them.

"Aye, bruh, do you got eyes on Ant or Pretty Girl?" I asked, still searching through the growing sea of faces.

"No... do you?" he asked.

"Dad, would you tell Mom to relax? It's not like I get to spend time with both of my parents every day," Ava complained.

I was turning back to respond to her when I caught sight of the front doors closing. A sudden chill ran down my spine, and I felt the familiar nudge to my subconscious that I'd gotten before shit had gone sideways at Flacco's place.

"Stuckey, something's wrong," I said.

"What's wrong, Nate?" Marissa asked.

Before I could voice my suspicions, the blaring sounds of the building's fire alarm screamed out. That was when I smelled smoke.

9

"It's a trap," I said, locking eyes with Marissa as the sounds of other people panicking grew louder around us.

The fear that sprang into Marissa's eyes tugged at my heart because I knew it wasn't for us. It was for our daughter.

"Get Ava out of here. Go out the way that we came in," I said.

"But-But what about all these people? I can't just leave, Nate. I'm the police chief. I can't just..."

"You're a mom *first*! Get our daughter out of here, and I'll try to find a way for these people to get out. Now go," I demanded, pushing her toward Ava.

"Dad!" Ava yelled.

"Go with your mom. I love you," I said, turning my back on both of them and heading into the crowd to try and calm the panic.

"The exits are chained shut, bruh, which makes this

banquet hall the world's biggest crockpot," Stuckey said through my earpiece.

"What about the windows?" I asked.

As soon as the words left my lips, the lady directly in front of me lost her head literally, courtesy of a well-placed .223 round. I never heard the echo from the shot that proved fatal to her, but the sound of glass breaking told me that the bullet had most likely travelled through the windows.

"Someone is shooting from outside, bruh. Stay away from the windows," I advised.

The screams started in earnest, and I saw two more bodies drop a few feet away from me.

"Oh, these niggas is serious," Stuckey said.

The sound of coughing was almost as loud as the screams, and I noticed that the smoke was getting thicker as it rolled through the room. I shifted my direction to take me out of the direct line of fire of the picture windows, but before I could move, I felt a hand on my elbow. When I turned and saw both Ava and her mom, my heart skidded to a stop in my chest. The fear that I'd seen in Marissa's eyes earlier was now full-blown terror, and Ava's were alight with the same wave of emotion.

"Stuckey, all the exits are blocked. We need a way out," I said, feeling fear's grip around my heart.

The thought of losing my child was in itself terrifying, but to have to witness it while knowing that I'd caused it would surely trap my soul in hell for all eternity.

"I'm working on it. The calvary is coming, but I doubt that we've got time to wait," Stuckey replied.

I heard more screams erupt as bodies hit the floor

missing their heads, and suddenly, the full-blown panic turned into a fast-moving stampede. The problem was that there was absolutely nowhere for anyone to run.

"You two stay with me!" I yelled over the deafening roar of the fire alarm and screams.

Marissa nodded as she passed me her black SIG Sauer P90 .45 and took Ava's arm. I quickly pulled the slide on the gun to chamber the first round to the party, and then I put my attention back on finding Stuckey.

"Bruh, where are you?" I asked.

"Just head toward the hole in the wall," he replied.

"What? What hole in the..."

Before I could get the question out of my mouth, a thunderous boom rocked the building, and then the north wall became a thing of the past. Suddenly, the night sky was visible, and the stampede that was trapped in stench of fear had a direction to escape. I grabbed Marissa's hand, and we moved like a three-car locomotive toward the smell of fresh air and the sounds of wailing sirens. As soon as we made it outside, we were surrounded by Stuckey and his men, who hustled us to waiting black Lincoln Navigators. We all hopped into one and vanished into the night as if we'd never been there.

"D-Dad, what the fuck just happened? Why would someone try to kill everyone at a charity event?!" Ava asked in a hysterical tone.

I didn't give an immediate answer, and before I could formulate a lie, Marissa had pulled her into her arms and was soothing her. I was trying to wrap my mind around what the fuck had just happened myself. I'd known that Ant was crazy, but turning a charity event into a full-blown kill box was some lunatic shit. The thought crossed my mind that the nigga had done all of that simply because he saw me talking to Pretty Girl, but logically, he'd had to have had that plan in motion long before we even got there. The sick bastard probably knew that he was gonna kill everyone when he'd made the bullshit Instagram video invitation. I doubted that he knew about Marissa's true history with me, or the daughter that we shared, but he would've taken pleasure in killing more of the people that I loved. The way that he'd moved tonight showed me just how far he would go in order to achieve the satisfaction of his revenge, and now it was time for me to get on the same page.

"Ayo, Stuck, we need to get them to a safe house," I said.

"Already ahead of you, bruh. We're going there right now," he replied from the front seat.

I spent the ride looking within my mind to find the most personal target that I could hit when it came to Ant. I wanted to deal him a crippling blow like he'd done me, but I knew that he'd be hiding the most obvious targets to keep them out of my range and off my radar. That meant that I needed a way to get to him without him seeing me coming. I was still rotating on that idea when we arrived at Stuckey's house, but I put it aside so that I could focus on all of us getting inside safely. Once that had been accomplished, I pulled my brother to the side while Marissa went into one of the spare bedrooms with Ava.

"Bruh, if you hadn't been there..."

"We ain't gonna think about that right now because it's irrelevant. I told you when we were kids that I'd always be there for you, and I meant that," he said sincerely.

I nodded once and tucked away the vulnerable emotions that I was feeling.

"We need a plan," I said.

"That nigga just tried to kill several federal agents and all types of people with political clout. There's nowhere safe for him to hide. He just became America's most wanted."

Part of me felt relief at Stuckey's assessment, but a bigger part of me wanted Ant's blood on my hands too much to let him fall into the hands of the law. Plus, the nigga wouldn't be dumb enough to let any law enforcement link him directly to what had happened tonight. In order for my soul to know peace, I was gonna have to kill this nigga myself. When I opened my mouth to tell Stuckey this truth, my phone started going off, causing me to pull it from my pocket. I wasn't surprised to see my wife calling because there was no doubt that tonight's events had made breaking news by now. Instead of answering her calls though, my eyes landed on half a dozen notifications that I had from Instagram. When I clicked on the first notification, I saw footage shot from inside the banquet hall, showing several different angles of the mayhem and carnage that I'd just barely survived. Each notification showed a different angle of the madness, and the sounds of the screams were absolutely as clear as I remembered. If that wasn't bad enough, the captions popping up were the knife to my heart. *#killedhismomandhermemory. #upthescore.*

"What's that?" Stuckey asked.

I passed him my phone while I struggled to regain my

composure and not let the tears of rage pooling in my eyes tumble down my face.

"What is it?" Marissa asked, walking up on me.

I didn't see Ava with her, and I was thankful for that because she'd been through enough tonight.

"There's video footage on IG from what we just went through, shot from inside the event. It's graphic," I warned.

I saw her eyes shift toward my brother, but she didn't move to view what he was looking at.

"What type of monster would do some shit like that and then post in on social media like it's something to be celebrated?" she asked.

I didn't have an answer to that question, so the only solace that I could offer was to open my arms and allow her to step into them. The shivering in her body was immediately evident, and that told me just how bad this shit had shaken her because I knew she was fearless. That was one of the main characteristics that made her so well suited for her job as D.C.'s chief of police. This threat was different though, and Ant was moving with the ruthlessness of a seasoned terrorist. Everyone knew that there was no reasoning with a nigga like that because the only thing that would stop him was a well-placed head shot.

"Nate, what are we gonna do?" she asked.

"Marissa, you should be good because I doubt that he'll make another attempt against the chief of police," Stuckey reasoned.

"Except he saw us together. And we know that he has footage of the inside of the banquet hall, so it's too dangerous to assume that he hasn't —_or won't —_put the pieces together," I said.

My words caused her to pull back and look up at me with the power of revelation glowing in the iris of her eyes.

"W-What are we gonna do?" she asked again.

The voice in my head was screaming, *I don't know,* until the quiet voice from within whispered a plan just crazy enough to work. It would go down as one of the oldest tricks in the book, but it would definitely change the game.

"We're gonna give Ant exactly what he wants," I replied.

"What the fuck you mean?" Stuckey asked.

"I'm talking about me dying... And Marissa, you're gonna be the one to kill me."

Both of them looked at me like I'd lost my muthafuckin mind, but I held up my hand to fight off their protests until I could explain the plan. I spoke uninterrupted for ten minutes, laying out the foundation of the plot still taking shape in my mind. When I was done laying out the bare bones, they added their input, and before we knew it, we'd pulled together something like perfection.

"This shit is crazy, Nate," Marissa said.

"I know, but it's gonna take some out of the box thinking to make a meaningful move against Ant," I replied.

"Are you sure that keeping Shytavia in the dark is the best way to do this though?" Stuckey asked.

The distaste that his question put in my mouth was all I needed to know that being dishonest with my wife was the hardest part of all of this. She would forgive me eventually but only if things worked out to perfection.

"The ends will justify the means," I replied.

"I agree. But it needs to be you who explains all of this to Ava because she deserves the complete truth," Marissa said, stepping aside and pointing toward the bedroom door that our daughter was behind.

"I'll set things in motion while you're doing that because we need to make this move before Ant has the chance to get anymore bright ideas," Stuckey said, passing me my phone back as he pulled his own out.

I hesitated, but Marissa quickly grabbed me by my hand and led me down the hallway. When she tried to turn my fingers loose, I clung to her like a kindergarten kid would his mom on his first day at a new school. When I looked at her, she nodded in understanding, and we entered the room together. Ava was laid across the bed, staring blankly at the ceiling, a long way from sleep.

"Sweetheart, I need to talk to you," I said.

She looked over at me, and then her eyes flashed to her mom before coming back to me. Slowly, she sat up and made room for us to sit beside her on the bed.

"You deserve a complete explanation with no omissions, and we both decided that I would be the one to give you that," I said.

"Which really means that Mom is making you tell the truth," Ava replied sarcastically.

I didn't take the bait. I just focused on the facts and began from the complicated history that I had with Pretty Girl. By the time that I was finished bringing Ava up to speed and laying out the plan that we'd just come up with, I could tell that all the gaps that she'd had before the banquet hall had now been filled.

"Okay, so... I die first?" Ava asked.

"Yeah," I replied, hating how it sounded.

"It'll keep you safe just in case someone has done the math and figured out that Nathan is your dad," Marissa said.

"Is-Is it gonna hurt?" she asked.

"Like a muthafucka," Marissa replied honestly.

Ava pondered that in silence for a few seconds, and then she gave a decisive nod.

"Okay, I'm with it, but Dad, you better shoot straight and know that no matter *what*, I'mma get my lick back one day."

I chuckled at what she said, pulling her into a bear hug until she was tapping me urgently to let her go. When I finally turned her loose, Stuckey was coming into the room with his phone out.

"This nigga is really playing his hand. He called a quick press conference and is condemning the actions of the cowards who attacked the banquet hall with all the passion of an experienced politician."

I took Stuckey's phone and watched as Ant gave an Oscar winning performance for the microphones and cameras in his face, but I wasn't fazed.

"Don't trip because what we're about to do will shed a little light on the shadows that he thinks he's safe in. Let's show everyone who he really is," I said.

"I'm with you, bruh," Stuckey replied, taking his phone back.

"It's settled then. Come on, daughter, it's time to die," I said, taking Ava by the hand.

10

"Are you ready to die?" I asked, invoking an extra menacing tone for the sake of the cameras aimed at me.

"P-Please don't! You don't have to do this! My mom is the chief of police and..."

I cut Ava's rehearsed pleas short by knocking her off of her feet with two shots center mass from the Taurus 9mm in my grip. I walked over to her fallen body and aimed the pistol at her again before turning my head to look over my left shoulder, directly at the phone in Stuckey's hand.

"Yo, Ant, this is how you up the score, you bitch ass nigga. You don't hide your hand. You just make the rest of the world fear it," I said, smirking as I fired the final kill shot in the direction of Ava's head.

Both Stuckey and Marissa lowered their phones, and then they went to work uploading the footage to IG and any other social media site that could broadcast it. The news stations would be next up. While they were doing that, I tucked the pistol into the front of my slacks, and I reached down to help Ava up off of the floor.

"You okay?" I asked.

"F-Fuck no! That shit was the worst pain that I ever experienced," she replied, climbing to her feet gingerly.

"Trust me, I know. I got hit without the benefit of a bulletproof vest though, so consider yourself fortunate," I said, pulling her into my arms.

"Alright, we're live," Stuckey said from behind me.

"First half of the hit job is complete. Where are the cops?" I asked.

"Waiting for my word to move in. There's only two of them, but they both will have body cameras on, and we won't shoot you until they're standing on either side of me. We're all gonna fire one shot after you raise your gun," Marissa explained, coming to stand beside me and Ava.

"None of you are packing hollow points or Black Talons, are you? This vest I got ain't standing up to that kinda pressure," I warned.

"Trust me, Nate, the last thing that I'mma do is give your ass the satisfaction of dying on me and leaving Ant to be *my* fucking problem," Marissa replied, smiling.

"How sweet of you," I said sarcastically.

"Alright, let's get this done so that we can get you and Ava underground," Stuckey said.

Marissa made the call to her people, and then she slipped out the back to meet up with them and position themselves in the alley.

"Dad, are you sure that this is gonna work?" Ava asked, looking up at me.

"Yeah, I'm sure. Ant wants me dead bad enough to

believe what the body cam footage will show the rest of the world. Once he thinks that I'm dead and gone, he'll let his guard down."

"How long will that take?" she asked.

"I don't know, sweetheart, as long as it takes. I know that you don't wanna go into hiding, and I'm sorry that we're putting you through this, but I can't let him take you from me too. I won't let that happen."

I could tell that she detested the idea of her hiding in seclusion somewhere unknown, but she still nodded in acceptance of the plan and my explanation.

"Marissa is in position. Let's do this," Stuckey said.

I kissed Ava on the forehead and stepped out of her embrace.

"I'll see you soon, sweetheart," I vowed softly.

She nodded bravely, but I saw the unshed tears in her eyes that were made brighter by the moon's luminosity lurking just outside the window. I wanted to stay and reassure her some more, but time was precious in this moment, and I knew that we had to seize the opportunity.

"The ambulance is gonna take you out of the city and into Maryland. The drivers are CIA, and they'll be taking you to some more members of the agency. I don't know where you're headed after that, but I'll be in touch with you sooner than later. Under no circumstances are you to contact Shytavia, and I'm being so serious about that because we need her reaction to your death to be authentic. You know that Ant is gonna be watching right up until your casket is laid into the ground or your ashes are spread somewhere," Stuckey said.

"I know, and I won't contact her until this is all over with, and I can actually get back to my old life."

"Give me your phone," he demanded, holding his hand out expectantly.

I gave it up without hesitation, despite my heart crying out for the sweet, melodic tones of my wife's voice to reach me.

"Alright, bruh, go out like a gangsta," he said, patting me on the back.

I started to cuss his ass out because I knew that the smirk on his face was due to the pain that he knew I was about to experience. It was the sadist in him. The only reason that I didn't call the nigga everything except Black Jesus was because if the roles were reversed, I'd definitely be laughing at his ass. It was part of our brotherly love. I pushed all of that from my mind though as I pulled my pistol back out and headed through the apartment to the back door. Once I got there, I took three deep breaths before I snatched the door open and rushed out into the night.

"Freeze, Ty! Drop the gun and give me my fucking daughter!" Marissa yelled convincingly.

I immediately froze and slowly turned to face her and the two cops flanking her.

"I told you that you'd get your daughter back when you brought my mom's killer to justice. Not a moment sooner," I replied.

"Anthony is a respectable businessman who just threw a lavish humanitarian event in honor of your mother. What proof do you have that he actually killed her or had her killed?" Marissa asked.

"The streets talk. All you gotta do is listen. Especially if you want your little girl back," I replied, taking a step forward.

"*Stop* fucking moving!" Marissa growled, gripping the gun out in front of her tighter.

"Nathan Ty, you're under arrest for kidnapping and..."

"I don't think so," I said, raising my gun and pointing it at the cop attempting to read me my Miranda rights.

Instantly, I saw flames light up the night sky, and a split second later, I was flying backwards through the air before landing hard on the cracked asphalt. The pain was so intense that I couldn't cry out or move, which played into the illusion we were selling about me being gunned down.

"Call an ambulance *now*!" Marissa yelled.

I heard the fake call go out, and then after a prolonged silence, I heard one of the cops say, "He's gone... turn the body cams off."

I still didn't move a muscle, just in case some innocent bystander happened along and couldn't resist being nosy. After a few minutes, the sounds of sirens getting louder as they approached could be heard. Within five minutes of being shot, I was scrapped up off the ground and loaded into the back of an ambulance, which then raced away at lifesaving speeds.

"Hurts like a bitch, huh?" Marissa asked as she helped me out of the bulletproof vest.

"I know for sure that Ava is gonna be bruised like a muthafucka because I can feel my skin changing colors," I said, wincing despite my best efforts to keep a straight face.

I was too busy mentally assessing my pain level to comment on Marissa chuckling at me, but I filed it to the back of my mind for later. As we rode on, the pain eased up a little, and I was able to refocus on the mission.

"Your forehead is creasing, which typically means that you're either worried or thinking extremely hard," I said.

"Don't think that you know me... but it's both. Everything looked real, and it should convince the world that you and our daughter are dead, but..."

"But what if it doesn't? Then we lose the complete element of surprise, but we don't lose it completely. As long as no one can pinpoint either mine or Ava's location then he'll just be chasing ghosts. It's our job to keep him too busy to do that. How will the body cam footage be released?" I asked.

"Both cops are gonna start the media leak in about an hour so that the footage of you killing Ava has time to circulate and take root."

"After that, what's your move?" I asked.

"A somber news conference where I'll take no questions and ask for time to mourn. What will you be doing?"

This part of the plan hadn't been discussed yet, and that was mainly because I'd still been trying to justify the demons that my plan had awoken. I'd tried to live by a code within my life and criminal activities, but I now knew that code had to go out the window because Ant had made this a fight without limitations. I accepted this, but I didn't know if Marissa would.

"Back at the banquet hall, Pretty Girl asked me to spare her life," I confessed.

"Okay, well now I'm definitely curious because that's seems like some shit that would make you spit in her face considering her choice in loyalty, not to mention the fact that she absolutely had to know that Ant killed your mom."

"She swears that she didn't know. Part of me believes her just because I know that niggas like Ant keep their moves a secret until it's too late for them to be compromised," I replied.

"Mmm, that sounds an awful lot like somebody I know," she said, giving me a pointed look.

I brushed her intended sarcasm off and stuck to the subject at hand.

"Anyways, Pretty Girl didn't ask me to spare her just because she didn't know about my mom. She asked me for the sake of her daughter."

"Daughter? She has a kid? Are you sure?" she asked skeptically.

"Yeah, but it's not just her kid. It's Ant's kid too."

"How old is she, Nate?"

I could tell by the look in her eyes and her tone of voice that she was about to draw a hard line with me about me not killing his kid.

"She's about Ava's age, maybe a little older," I replied.

"Okay. Well, I know that you've got a huge heart when it comes to the people that you love, but I have a bad feeling that this conversation ain't about you granting anyone amnesty."

"Nah, we're beyond that at this point, but I'm not gonna kill her," I said.

"So, what's your plan?"

"I'm gonna wait until the time is right, and then I'm gonna leverage her to bring that bitch made nigga to his knees," I replied honestly.

Marissa didn't verbally reply, but I could see the disapproval crystalize in her eyes that were trying to burn a hole through my retinas. We rode in silence for a full ten minutes before she finally spoke again.

"I don't like it, Nathan."

"You made that perfectly clear already," I said sarcastically.

She gave me an openhanded love tap to the chest, but the pain that shot through me almost made me levitate off the gurney like a cat surprised by a cucumber.

"Dammit, stop!" I growled, shooting daggers at her with my eyes.

"You're in no condition to be a smartass, and I felt the need to remind you of that. Now, like I was saying, I don't like your diabolical plan, but I get it. I need you to make me a promise right here and now though."

"What do you want?" I asked, still trying to catch my breath around the pain.

"I want you to promise me that under no circumstances are you gonna kill this girl."

"You would ask me that after you AND our daughter barely escaped a fiery death courtesy of her father not long ago?" I asked.

"Yes, because that was *his* doing. That girl is just as innocent as Ava is, and this is the one demand that I won't budge on. Not if you expect me and Ava to still be a part of your life when this is all over."

The look on her face in this moment was one that I was painfully familiar with because it was pure stubbornness and determination. I'd battled her before when this was the approach that she took, but the harder I fought, the more her inner red head devil showed his ass. I didn't have the time or strength to fight her now, and we both knew it.

"I won't kill her. I promise," I vowed.

She stared at me hard for a few moments, and then slowly the heat in her eyes died down. We spent the rest of the remaining twenty minutes going over the plan for us to keep in contact, even though neither of us knew when we'd be face to face again. When the ambulance finally came to a stop, we were both caught up in an awkward silence, not wanting to say goodbye but slowly acknowledging that, for whatever reason, this could be our last moments together —_at least in this lifetime.

"I love you, Nate... And in case I never said it before, I wanna thank you for always being there to catch me when I fell."

"Ditto, sexy red," I replied, taking her hand and smiling at her.

She leaned down and gave me a quick kiss on the lips, and then she got up to open the back doors to the ambulance. By the time I struggled into a sitting position, there were four men, two white and two Black, wearing identical black suits, standing a few feet away from the door. Marissa helped me down, and we shared a long hug full of historical reference before I finally pulled back and followed my handlers to the blacked-out Yukon Denali idling nearby. We loaded up and vanished into the night at a high rate of speed.

"Where are we headed?" I asked the Black guy sitting on the bench seat in the back with me.

In response to my question, he handed me a phone that started ringing immediately.

"Hello?" I answered cautiously.

"Well, it's good to know that some of the D.C. cops can still shoot straight. How are you feeling?" Stuckey asked.

"Like when you catch the muthafucka driving the truck that smacked my ass, I'mma fuck his *whole* week up."

My response made him laugh, despite how serious I felt. I knew that this was Ant's fault though, and you best believe that my black ass was keeping score.

"Don't worry. I'll make sure that you've got something for the pain when you get where you're going," he promised.

"And where exactly am I going?"

"Well, that depends on you and what it is that you want. Do you simply want revenge in the form of killing Ant, or do you wanna up the score by breaking him until he wants to take his own life?" he asked seriously.

His question threw me off a little, but the answer was an easy one.

"I wanna break that nigga, bruh," I replied.

"Yeah, that's what I thought you'd say. For that reason, your first stop is to a highly respected plastic surgeon. It's time to really make you invisible."

CHAPTER 11

SIX MONTHS LATER

"Can I help you?"

"No, I was just admiring this picture. The contrast of dark to light gives the photo a gritty feeling, a texture that most people can't capture unless they have a great eye," I replied, still gazing at the image on the wall.

"You obviously have a great eye yourself. Are you a photographer?"

"Nah, I'm just an admirer. What about you?" I asked.

"Actually, I took this picture," she replied, gesturing toward the work of art that I was standing in front of.

The information that she'd just divulged was what I'd known all along and the reason that I'd come into this art gallery in downtown San Francisco every day this week. Joy Robinson, aka Miss Joy, was something of a well-known photographer on the West Coast, even though most people felt like she was meant to be in front of the camera. Her beauty in person severely outweighed the photos that I'd seen of her. Her skin tone was honey golden and flawless, which perfectly complimented the golden dreadlocks that ran down to the middle of her back. She couldn't have been more than 5'6", and her curves added up to about one hundred fifty pounds of thickness by my mental calculation. Gorgeous was the word that came to mind, and with the new face the surgeon blessed me with, I knew that she was undoubtedly viewing me the same way. Now that the healing was done in regard to the surgical scars, I knew that I could give a young Morris Chestnut a run for his money and his bitch. When I turned to face her, I could see the pulse quicken in her neck, and it filled me with the thirst of a vampire.

"So, you're the infamous Miss Joy?" I asked, smiling seductively.

"I don't know about infamous, and you don't gotta call me Miss, but yeah, my name is Joy. And you are?"

"I'm Angelo, but my friends call me Lo," I replied, extending my hand to her.

She took it, and her grip was firm, despite the softness of her hand.

"I'll call you Angelo since we just met."

"Hmm... sounds so formal coming from your mouth, and I'm not sure how I feel about that. Maybe we should get to know each other better," I suggested, still smiling.

"Ohhh, so you're cute and dangerous with the smooth talk. Un uh, my mama told me about men like you," she replied, laughing.

"She told you... or she warned you?"

"Both! But she knows that I'mma whole grown ass woman who will make her own decisions," she said.

"Mmm, okay, so what's your decision on joining me for a cup of coffee? No pressure."

"Oh, really, no pressure, huh? You just gonna put me on the spot like that while I'm out here in these streets trying to get my money right? But it's *no* pressure though," she said, laughing again.

The sound of her laughter wasn't just hypnotic. It was intoxicating like that first hit of fentanyl. I allowed it to wash over me like a waterfall in an exotic place while making sure to stare at her with an intensity that spoke volumes beyond words.

"I'm not trying to interrupt your paper chase in the slightest, so the rain check is yours if you want it," I offered.

I could see her carefully contemplating my offer, and the adventure swimming in her light brown eyes told me which way she was leaning in regard to a decision. This was a look that I knew well but from a different lifetime.

"I'm open to compromise if you are."

"I'm listening," I replied, turning to face her fully.

"Well, I'm done with business today, and I'm actually waiting on a buyer to come and collect three of my pictures, this one here that you're admiring and two others on different walls, but after that, I was planning to go get something to eat. If you'd like to join me..."

The smile that she gave me was somewhat shy, and it gave her beauty an innocent appeal that caused my heart to stutter a little from a nostalgic memory.

"Do you always ask strange men out to dinner?" I asked.

"Absolutely-the fuck-not but you're not exactly a

stranger, are you? I mean, you have been coming in here for the past week, even if it was just to window shop," she replied, tilting her head to the side and giving me a mischievous smile.

"Okay, I see that I wasn't as inconspicuous as I'd thought, but you're only partially correct in your observation."

"Oh, really? Well, please correct me where I'm wrong," she said sassily.

In response, I reached into my pocket and pulled out a handwritten receipt, which I handed to her. She looked at it and laughed.

"Well played. So, *you're* the owner I'm waiting on to collect these pieces. The narcissist in me believes that you went through all of this just to meet me, but honestly, you don't seem like the type," she said.

I laughed softly while shaking my head negatively.

"While I admit that you're an exceptionally beautiful woman, I admit that my interest in your photographs was strictly my business savvy at work. I acquired these pieces knowing that I've got buyers who'll jump at the chance to own them —_when and if I decide to put them on the market."

"Ah, so you're an art dealer?" she asked.

"I wouldn't classify it strictly as art that I collect because I live to acquire the finest things that the world has to offer. Some things have a price... and others are simply priceless," I replied, giving her a look to match the seductive smile on my face.

She didn't reply verbally, but I definitely saw the deep

breath she'd taken as the fingers on her left hand subconsciously found their way into her hair.

"Well, uh, I appreciate your business. I've built a nice buzz in the three years that I've been out here, but I'm still hungry."

"I like that type of drive in a woman. As for the hungry part, I believe that we can remedy that just as soon as you pass along this address for the pieces to be delivered to," I said, reaching into my pocket and producing a slip of paper with a rented storage locker's information on it.

She took it and paired it with the receipt.

"I'll take care of this and come right back."

I nodded and turned back to stare at the picture of the little Black boy sitting on the steps of a project building in some inner city. Despite my nefarious intentions, I really did appreciate the quiet beauty that Joy was able to capture through a photo lens, and this picture spoke to the boy inside of me. I knew the hurt and hunger in his eyes intimately because it was what had motivated me to become an entrepreneur in my former life. My acquisition of the art was a sound business investment, but that wasn't the only reason that I'd made the purchase. After a quick glance around, I pulled my phone out of my pocket and sent a quick text that read 'contact made'. I didn't wait for a response; I just put the phone back into my pocket and continued to strategize my next move in my mind. A few moments later, Joy was back by my side, handing me my papers back.

"The pieces will be delivered within the hour. Do you need to oversee the packing and shipping before we head to dinner?" she asked.

"No, I trust that your business runs smoothly without my micromanaging skills. Plus, there's no need to worry about the valuable art when I've got the priceless artist."

"You ain't got me yet," she replied, walking away from me and throwing a quick glance over her shoulder in my direction.

I followed her without hesitation, and she led me to the parking lot on the side of the building.

"Do you know where you wanna go?" she asked.

"Take me to your favorite restaurant."

I watched her think about it for a second as the burnt orange sky made its transition to a dusky purple all around us. Even though she was only wearing some red jean shorts with an off the shoulder white halter top paired with wedged sandals, she looked runway ready. I wasn't any type of artist or photographer, but I'd pay my weight in gold for this picture of her in this moment.

"I'm up for some hibachi, and I know the perfect Japanese restaurant. You wanna follow me in your car, or I can just bring you back here afterwards," she said.

"That's me right there, and I'll leave the travel decisions up to you," I replied, pointing to the space that I was parked in.

Her eyes followed my gesture, and I saw the excitement suddenly fill them when she saw my black-on-black Suzuki GSX-R 1300 motorcycle.

"Oh, you're definitely a nigga that my mama warned me about," she said, laughing.

"Really? Just because I ride a motorcycle?"

"Absolutely! She told me about this man that she'd

fallen for once upon a time, and she described him as a 'threat to her sanity'," she replied.

"All of that just because he drove a bike though?"

Even in the fast-approaching darkness, I could see the beauty of her blush, and it took all of my effort not to laugh out loud.

"It-It wasn't just the motorcycle. She said that he took her for a ride, fucking her mind with amazing conversation, and before she knew it, he was fucking her with a hook in his dick that made her toes curl while she prayed for sin," she said, locking eyes with me.

I paused before speaking, just to let the anticipation build, and then, I took a small step toward her.

"So... do you wanna ride?" I asked.

The noise of passing traffic was instantly drowned out by the sound of her swallowing around the lump in her throat, and I couldn't suppress the smile that popped up on my face.

"I-I don't do shit like this."

"But?" I asked, waiting for her to verbalize her decision.

It took her a few moments to finally admit to herself what we both knew already, and then, she pulled her phone out of her pocket.

"Here's the address."

I pulled my phone out, unlocked it, and tapped against hers to transfer the information between us. I immediately recognized the location, but I didn't let my face betray that knowledge.

"Come on," I said, taking her by the hand and leading her over to my bike.

I passed her my helmet, and while she put it on, I linked my phone to my bike's GPS and put my Bluetooth in so that I could put my phone back in my pocket. With that complete, I hopped on the bike and waited for her to climb on behind me.

"Hold on... tight," I instructed.

She followed my directions without pause or hesitation, and I wasted no time cranking the bike up and pulling off. Twenty minutes later, we pulled up in front of a high rise building that looked as if it extended straight up into the clouds.

"This is a restaurant?" I asked, feigning innocence.

"Give me your keys," she demanded, hopping off the bike.

I turned the bike off, passed her my key, and watched as she took the helmet off her head while walking toward the valet. They exchanged a few words, and then she motioned me over.

"It'll be parked in a reserved spot. Come on," she said, holding out her hand.

I took it, and she led me inside, straight to a bank of elevators that took us up to the twenty-seventh floor. Again, she led me, down the hall, and she didn't stop until we were standing in front of the door that I knew belonged to her apartment. I didn't say a word, and neither did she as she placed her palm on the scanner by the door which allowed us entrance. I could feel her nervousness in her trembling fingers, but she pulled me inside the apartment like a woman on a mission.

"This is nice. I bet it cost..."

"Stop talking," she demanded huskily, shoving me up against the door hard enough to shut it behind us.

I didn't get the chance to utter another word anyway because her mouth was instantly on mine, hot and insistent like my breath was her air. For a second, my brain scrambled as thoughts of my wife pushed to the forefront, dragging guilt in their wake and making me question what the fuck I was about to do. I'd never cheated on my wife, and I'd always vowed to never be that guy, but this wasn't about pleasure. This was strictly about standing on bidness. When her hands started pulling on my shirt, I allowed her to strip me out of it, and then I returned the favor. The way that her titties popped free of the cotton fabric and stood up at attention without a bra, courtesy of youth and good DNA, made my mouth water. Without thought, I lifted her off of her feet by her firm ass cheeks and pulled her to me until I could capture one of her dark brown nipples in my mouth.

"Shit," she moaned, holding on to my head.

I spent a few moments giving both of her titties equal attention before I finally lowered her back to her feet. Her fingers immediately went to work on my jeans as my own fingers synchronized with her to make quick work of her shorts, and seconds later, we were both naked.

"Oh, God, you got the hook too," she said weakly, taking my dick in her hand and stroking it lovingly.

"Don't panic... yet," I whispered before reclaiming her mouth with my own.

I spun her into the nearest wall and lifted her into the air while keeping her back braced against the smooth, hard surface for balance.

"Condom," she mumbled.

"Next round," I replied, using my hand to guide my dick up in between her juicy pussy lips.

Before I could make the initial plunge, the silent night came alive with sounds of a ringing phone. We both froze like two teenagers getting caught.

"Do-Do you need to get that?" I asked, fighting to control my raging hormones.

"I hope not but wait until the answering machine catches it."

After four rings, it stopped, and the night was once again silent except for the sounds of our labored breathing.

"Alexa, play message," she commanded.

"You have... one message..."

"Joy, this is your mom, and I'm just checking on you. Call me when you get this."

"Do you need to take care of that right now?" I asked, smiling.

"No disrespect but Diamond can wait. Just fuck me."

I pushed my dick up inside her with enough force to have me standing on my tiptoes. The breath expelled from her lungs, sounding like oxygen feeding a raging fire through a broken window. By the time I hit her with my second stroke, I could feel her nails digging into my skin as her grip tightened around my shoulders simultaneously with her pussy's grip clutching me. This wasn't a love making session, and I wasn't about to turn it into one. I continued to pound dick into her, nailing her to the wall like one of her own famous works of art while watching the beautiful canvas of her face register passion and pleasure. The way that she bit her lip in uncontrollable ecstasy sent another shock of nostalgia to my brain that only added to my determination to slay her. Without taking my dick out of her, I moved her from the wall to the couch and laid her down.

"Rub your clit," I demanded breathlessly as I put both of her legs on my shoulders, altering the angle of our alignment.

As soon as her fingers took the walk within her secret garden, I started applying hypnotic pressure with strokes that sent her eyes to vacation with her brain. I intended to make her mine by taking her soul, and within minutes, an orgasm rolled through her with enough force to shift the tectonic plates that ran beneath San Francisco. I wanted to cause that earthquake. I didn't change speed or technique as I fucked her through the storm and right into the aftermath of the hurricane second climax that ripped her body apart metaphorically. The sounds of her whimpering in delirious bliss fed my ego and only increased the stamina flowing throughout me. I could feel my own climax pressing on my spine, and my nerve endings were tingling at the prospect of fulfillment, but I held out a little while longer. I slowed down the tempo and gave her body a few moments to rebuild, selling the illusion that the storm had passed, and then I hit her with the dope dick. I fed her long strokes steadily, using the hook that she feared to knock down the last walls of her sanity as she fell from the heights beyond Heaven.

"L-Lo-Looo," she sang out in high pitch tones.

"I'm here," I moaned, feeling my cum shoot inside her like .223 rounds.

I didn't stop pumping inside of her until my eyes could

barely stay open, and then I laid halfway on top of her, trying to catch my breath. Neither of us spoke because all we could do was gulp down breaths that tasted like sex and satisfaction. It took at least five minutes before I was able to lift myself up and out of her, and I almost didn't make it because her pussy's punishing grip was still active.

"You said I was dangerous, but now I know that you were just rocking me to sleep," I said, chuckling as I sat beside her on the couch.

"Nigga, please! I'm embarrassed by how you just fucked me and simultaneously fucked it up for any man who ever thought he ever has a chance after you."

Pride caused me to pull her toward me until we were cuddling lazily together. I ran my fingers through her locs while gently massaging her scalp until I heard her breathing drop low enough to signal sleep had claimed her. I waited a few more minutes before moving to stand up, and then I scooped her up into my arms. I carried her down the hallway, passing an empty spare bedroom, until I arrived at the master suite. It was easy to tell that she was a girly girl based upon the decorations in various shades of pink, but I didn't focus on that as much as I did the king-sized bed in the middle of the room. After I laid her down, I stood there for a moment to see if she was gonna wake up, and then I tiptoed out of the room back in the direction I'd come. The guilt that I was still struggling to suppress was whispering to me that I needed to put my clothes on and get the fuck out. In my heart, I knew it was too late to turn back now though. I put my boxer briefs back on and grabbed my phone out of my jeans pocket before making my way outside on the balcony. The city was absolutely mesmerizing from this view, but my focus was on the call that I had to make.

"What's goody, bruh?" Stuckey answered.

"Shit, the pussy is. I can't even lie, my nigga."

"Damn, you already made it that far?" he asked, sounding surprised.

"I'm light weight as surprised as you are, bruh, but slim is aggressive just like her mama."

My response made him chuckle.

"Okay, so did you put it down proper?" he asked.

"Next question. She's tucked in bed right now, bout to fuck her pillow up wit big drool," I bragged.

"Okay, okay, excuse me for doubting your skills. Seriously though, how are you really doing?"

I took a moment to really evaluate his question, allowing the truth to step forward around the lies I'd been continuously telling myself.

"Honestly, bruh, now that I've made it this far, it's hitting home how fucking crazy all of this is. I mean, I love Tay, and I know that she's been in literal hell for the past six months while I've been consumed by revenge. It's not that I feel guilt for fucking Diamond and Ant's daughter; it's just that I'd rather be fucking my wife," I replied truthfully.

"I hear you, bruh. If it's any consolation, I've been checking on Tay and Peanut, just to make sure that they're straight in North Carolina, and they're good. She's stronger than you think, and Peanut is still too young to know what's going on. Hopefully you'll be back with him before he realizes you were ever gone."

"I hope you're right, but that depends on Ant. What's

the latest?" I asked, switching gears back to the business at hand.

"He's moving like a nigga with no worries, which makes me wanna blow his muthafuckin brains all over his pretty Bentley. I know that we're playing the long game though, so what's your next move?"

I opened my mouth to answer, but I paused at the sight of Joy's naked body headed in my direction.

"I'mma make her fall in love and then shatter her parents' soul," I replied, hanging up the phone as she opened the sliding glass door.

"Let me guess. You were just on the phone bragging to your boys about how you fucked me to sleep," she said, giving me a half smile.

"Sorry to disappoint you, but I'm a whole grown ass man, sweetheart, which means that I don't need to brag on my dick. I just need to serve you righteously."

"Mmm, I like the sound of that," she replied, stepping outside and closing the distance between us.

"I was actually gonna order some food since we never made it to the restaurant, but now I've got a better idea," I said, pulling her into my arms.

"Do tell."

"How about I cook for you?" I suggested.

"Wait, you cook? Ain't no way I'm believing that," she replied, laughing.

"Why is that so hard to believe?"

"Because a nigga as fine as you, that fucks like he invented sex, *can't* know how to feed a bitch too! If that was the case then you would've *been* married by now, and I'd be plotting on how to kill your wife or convince her that I'd make the perfect sister wife," she said, smiling.

Her mentioning marriage made my heart lurch in my chest, but I kept my poker face on and continued to bury the guilt.

"Come with me and let me show you this miracle that you can't believe," I said, taking her by the hand and leading her back inside.

I found the kitchen, deposited her on a bar stool at the center island, and then I set about finding something to whip up to impress her. The thought in my mind already was that breakfast would be the fastest meal I could make, and once I saw what I was working with, I was able to get busy.

"So, I know this is working in reverse chronological order, but why don't you tell me more about yourself?" I stated, glancing at her briefly over my shoulder.

"Do you really wanna know, or is this your polite way of not slut shaming me for fucking you before the first date?"

The question was asked with a lighthearted tone, but my intuitiveness allowed me to detect the slightly insecure current hidden within her words. This was the part in the movie where the young nigga would fumble the ball, but I was a seasoned vet in the art of seduction. I sat the food on the counter, and then I walked around the center island until I was standing right in front of her. With slow and deliberate movements, I took her face into my hands and kissed her with all the tenderness I knew that she imagined true love to hold. When I pulled back, her eyes were closed, and then they fluttered open in a way that laid bare all the vulnerability she undoubtedly wanted to hide from the world.

"I wanna get to know you on all levels, not just the physical, because I know that you're even more amazing after the sweat dries," I said softly, making sure to stare at her long enough to leave a lasting impression.

She blushed beautifully, but all I really saw was the fishhook burrowing deeper into her jaw making it impossible for her to get away. That made me smile. The sound of the phone ringing interrupted our moment, but I knew that the damage was done.

I went back to preparing a breakfast of French toast, eggs, and sausage while she picked up the phone off of the counter.

"Yes, Mother?" she answered.

My back was to her at this point, so she couldn't see the evil smile stretching across my face.

"Yes, I know that you called me earlier, but I was busy... I was getting that dick that you warned me about all my life if you must know," she said, laughing loudly.

I spun around to face her with genuine shock contorting my features because I hadn't expected her to be so damn bold. She smiled at me mischievously and gave me a quick wink before she turned her attention back to the conversation.

"Ma, you don't need to know who I'm fucking, and when there's something substantial to tell you, I'll tell you. For now, I'd just like to get back to watching this beautiful, Black man cook for me. Goodnight, Mother."

I could hear Diamond yelling something as Joy pulled

the phone from her ear, but I turned my attention back to the food prep.

"You and your mom seem to have a… close relationship."

"We do. That's my bitch for real, and we talk about everything. I just wasn't about to give her details about your dick game where you could hear it and let it go to your head," she replied.

"Go to my head? Sweetheart, please. That was only the first round. I'm planning to feed you, and then fuck you until you're too weak to walk, and *then* you can pray to this dick like it's your newfound religious item."

"Mmph, pray for me, Lord," she mumbled under her breath.

I laughed at that, and then I consciously shifted the conversation back to the previous topic.

"So... are you gonna tell me more about you, or do I gotta get your mama back on the phone?" I asked.

"Oh, fuck no! I love my mama, but she's like a bloodhound when it comes to smelling good dick on a nigga, and I'm *not* sharing you."

"I like the possessive tone in your voice," I replied, chuckling.

"Good, get used to it. Back to me though... Well, I'm originally from Virginia, but I got the fuck outta dodge as soon as I could. I've got a couple of half siblings, but I don't really know about them because they're on my father's side of the family. My dad is a businessman, and my mom is a 'kept lady', but it works for them. I don't care as long as my credit cards don't get declined because only then would their shit become my problem. Even though I come from money, I still want to leave my mark on the world independently. It's the Leo in me, so I don't apologize for it. I've been out here on the West Coast long enough to fall in love with the California sunshine, and I don't go back east unless someone has a gun to my head. I *love* my work. I like to play as hard as I work, but that don't mean that I'm free with this good pussy because I'm not. You're only the third man I've been with."

Her revelation stopped my movements and made me look at her.

"Sweetheart, I never thought that you were free with the pussy, and I hope you know that the value of you shines brightly without you having to say a word. I wasn't attracted to you for the mere sake of your outer beauty because your energy carries so much more sex appeal," I stated.

She nodded her head in appreciation, and I could tell by the light in her eyes that the insecurity that she was battling was starting to fade. I didn't wanna put her on the spot, so I got back to work fixing our food.

"I think that it's your turn to tell me about yourself now, Lo."

"Oh, so we've moved past you calling me Angelo?" I asked, chuckling.

"Most *definitely*! You made me cum on that dick harder than I ever have, so we're *way* beyond friends, my nigga."

"Agreed. What do you wanna know?" I asked.

"Everything, but we can start with the basics for now."

I thought about how much truth to merge with lies in my cover story.

"Okay, well, I'm from the east coast as well, Baltimore,

Maryland to be exact. I'm a well-rounded huslta, but money don't mean shit without someone to celebrate happiness with. In my youth, I was something like a whore, but I've outgrown that part, and I'm more of a relationship type guy now. No pressure."

"Yeah, the last time that you said, 'no pressure', I ended up with my legs wrapped around you," she said.

We both laughed at the truth in that, and I knew where this was headed.

"I understand if you're not the relationship type. I mean, you're a beautiful, young woman with the world at her feet."

"That I am... but I could be convinced to settle down if the right man came along," she replied coyly.

"The right man, huh? Tell me what that looks like in your mind."

"The easy answer would be to say *you*, but... I don't know if that's true yet. I'm willing to give you until sunrise to convince me though," she said.

"Challenge accepted. Now I suggest that you eat all of your food because you're gonna need your energy."

CHAPTER 12

ONE MONTH LATER

"You wanna watch a movie?" I asked, looking at her from my prone position of laying on the couch with my head in her lap.

"Wow, that's rare. Normally you're suggesting that we make our own movies."

"That's your fault! I've been hooked ever since I saw how amazing you looked after we made the first one," I said, smiling at her.

"Hooked? Was that a dick reference?"

"If you want it to be," I countered, taking her hand and slowly kissing her fingertips.

Her breathing hit a fast shift like the brand-new Dodge Red Eye she'd bought for me last week, and I loved knowing that I had this power over her. After that first all-night fuck fest, Joy and I had been glued to the pelvis and virtually inseparable, making my plan flawless at this point. I was just waiting on one more piece to fall into place before my plan went from dormant to fully active.

"Baby, don't start because you know that if you start to feed me that good dick then I'm gonna want to finish all my food."

"Mmm, won't that make your mama proud," I said, continuing with my seduction.

The moan that escaped her throat sounded like submission, which meant that I had her right where I wanted her.

"I'll let you live for now but only because there's something that I wanna talk to you about. A business proposition," I said.

"Yes. Whatever it is, the answer is yes," she replied readily.

I laughed as I lowered her hand from my mouth and placed it on my heart.

"I want you to hear me out first because you might think what I'm about to suggest will damage your brand, but I think it'll send you into the stratosphere."

"Okay, well, I like the sound of the last part, but now you've got me wondering," she said, chuckling nervously.

"I know that I'm not a photographer in any sense of the word, but even you said that I took some good, provocative still shots of your naked beauty. So, I was thinking we take those, and our video sexual exploits, and open an OnlyFans page. I predict that we'll damn near break the site with your sexy self."

I could tell by the look in her face that she was surprised by what I was suggesting, but it didn't look like she was mad.

"OnlyFans, huh? It's crazy that you say that because I remember when Bhad Bhabie posted about how much she earned in her first year of doing OnlyFans. I swore that I was in the wrong business. What's kept me from doing it was hearing my parents' mouth and not having anyone that I trusted enough to do it with me," she said.

"I won't speak on the parental issue because I don't know them or how they'll react, but I promise that I'll always protect you from anyone, including them. The only question is do you trust me?"

The way that she smiled down at me said the words that I knew were about to flow from in between her soft lips, but before she could speak, the doorbell ringing filled the air.

"You expecting someone?" I asked, sitting up and looking in the direction of the front door.

"No, but it's probably my friend, Hannah, that works at the gallery with me. I haven't exactly been pulling my weight since you and I turned my apartment into a fuck palace," she replied, getting up and going toward the door.

I didn't go with her, but my ears were perked up like any good guard dog's should be. I heard her open the door, and then I heard something that made my heart beat faster.

"Mom? What-What are you doing here?" Joy asked, sounding more than a little surprised.

"You've been avoiding me more than usual, so I thought that it was time for me to pop up on that ass and make sure that your mystery man hadn't fucked you to death," Pretty Girl replied.

"Oh, my God, *Shhh!* Do *not* embarrass me," Joy said, already sounding mortified.

"I won't. Now, where is he?"

I didn't hear Joy's response, but the sound of the door closing reached my ears moments before Pretty Girl strutted into the room ahead of her daughter. Our eyes locked, but there was no hint of recognition in hers, only the look of curious appraisal.

"So, you're the nigga trying to turn my daughter out," she said, stopping a few feet away from me.

I looked back-and-forth between the two women intentionally, affixing my face with a confused expression.

"I'm sorry, but you must have me confused because I don't know your daughter. I'm with your sister," I said, nodding toward Joy.

"No, bae, this is my mom, Di..."

"Pretty Girl is what I go by," she said, stepping forward to give me her delicate hand.

Instinctively, I started to kiss her hand the same way I had the first time that we met a lifetime ago, but I resisted the temptation because I didn't need that memory resurfacing. Instead, I just shook her hand and let it go.

"Hi, my name is Angelo."

"Angelo, huh? Is that what my daughter calls you?"

"With all due respect, whatever she calls me is between me, her, and these four walls," I replied cooly.

From the corner of my eye, I saw the smirk pop up on Joy's face, but Pretty Girl was giving me a look of heated agitation. I knew that she wasn't used to getting shut down, especially not by a man.

"I bet that these walls could talk, but you're right; it's not my business. Tell me, Angelo, what are your intentions with my daughter?"

"Come on, Ma. Don't start..."

"It's okay, sweetheart. I can handle it. Pretty Girl, are you asking me what I want from Joy?"

"That's exactly what I'm asking you."

"Well, that answer is simple. I want *everything*. I want her mind, body, soul, and spirit. I want her to be so lost within our love that she'd war with God Almighty to keep it. I want her *life* if I demanded that she sacrifice it... Does that answer your question?" I asked, standing up and taking a step toward Pretty Girl.

Joy's jaw had gone slack, and her mouth was hanging open, but she hadn't uttered a word yet.

"Love? You *think* that you love my daughter after a month of fucking and playing house?"

"No, I loved her before that because I fell in love with the way that she saw the world. Her pictures showed me her soul, and any woman who can move me that deeply without speaking a word to me is a woman that I was made to worship," I replied, shifting my attention to Joy.

The tears that appeared in her eyes were clearly unexpected, and they spilled onto her cheeks without her feeling the need to check them. As the seconds moved on, I quickly realized that Pretty Girl was speechless, but I intentionally ignored her because I wanted the full power of my words to consume Joy. I sidestepped her mom and moved in to place a gentle kiss on her lips.

"I'll let you two catch up," I said softly before making my way toward the bedroom.

I didn't actually go into the bedroom though. I actually hid out of sight so that I could eavesdrop undetected.

"Well, uh, I can see why you like him," Pretty Girl stammered.

"I don't just like him, Ma. I love him. I've been falling

in love with him, but I've been too scared to say shit because I didn't wanna scare him off."

"A man like that don't scare easily... He kinda reminds me of someone that I knew a long time ago," Pretty Girl said.

I could hear the wistful sentiment in her tone, and it pulled at my conscience, but I shut the door on it by remembering my mother's face before Ant's goons killed her. There wasn't room to feel sorry for anyone anymore.

"I know that he don't remind you of Daddy because I can promise you that him and Angelo are nothing alike. Speaking of Daddy though, where is he because I *know* he didn't let you fly to the West Coast by yourself."

"Don't make it sound like your dad got some type of fucking leash on me because I still got a mind of my own," Pretty Girl said defensively.

"I'm not saying that you don't have your own mind, Mama. I'm just saying that I know how my daddy is."

"Whatever. He made the trip out here, but he's in L.A. visiting his mother and brother," Pretty Girl replied.

"I was just down there a few months ago because I had an exhibit on display, and I stopped in to check on her and Uncle Darnell. They were fine, except for the cabin fever," Joy said.

"Cabin fever? Shit, you make it sound like they live in a one room shack instead of a seven-bedroom mansion in Brentwood."

"You know what I mean, Ma. Dad don't allow them to hardly go anywhere, and when they do, it's with a presidential motorcade. The only privacy that Grandma gets is physical therapy for her bad back, and if she wasn't getting dick from her therapist, she might kill herself," Joy replied.

"First of all, eww. Secondly, your dad is just trying to keep them safe, and your grandma and uncle know that. It was the tradeoff that they agreed to in order to have their wants and needs taken care of, so believe me when I tell you that they're fine."

I'd heard enough to be able to formulate a quick plan, and so I moved down the hallway, through the bedroom, and into the master bathroom. After I turned the shower on, I pulled my phone out and quickly called Stuckey.

"Bruh, I got a lead that I need you to check on right quick," I said.

"What's shaking?"

"This nigga, Ant, is hiding his mom and brother in L.A. They're sitting pretty in a mansion in Brentwood. I don't know his mother's name, but I know that his brother's name is Darnell," I replied.

"Okay, I'll find them. What do you want me to do with them once I have their location?"

I pondered for a moment on what poetic justice would look like, and once the right idea drifted up from my subconscious, I felt the smile spreading across my face.

"Snatch them up and send them to Oscar. I'm about to leave now and head in that direction," I said.

"Do I even want to know why you're involving crazy ass Oscar?"

"Probably not, but sooner than later, you'll find out. Everyone will," I replied, disconnecting the call.

I slid my phone back into the pocket of my shorts and then turned the shower off before walking out of the bathroom. I'd basically been living out of a duffle bag for the last month that I'd spent under Joy's roof, so it didn't take me long to throw my clothes in the bag. I wasn't taking everything because I fully intended to come back, but I took enough to create the subconscious insecurity within that would occupy her brain until I returned. Once I was packed, I headed back out into the living room. As soon as I walked in, the conversation ceased, and I saw the confused fear cloud Joy's eyes and contort her face.

"Wh-Where are you going?" she asked, quickly rising to her feet and crossing to where I stood.

"I'm gonna go past my place and get some more clothes, but first, I'mma check on some business stuff. That'll give you and your mom time to catch up, and I'll be back sometime tomorrow."

"T-Tomorrow? So, you won't be spending the night here?" she asked in a slightly panicked tone.

My eyes flickered over toward Pretty Girl before coming back to Joy, and then I stepped closer so that I could put my lips to her ear.

"I'm trying to make a good impression, bae, plus I've got a surprise for you. I just need you to trust me," I whispered before pulling back so that I could look down into her eyes.

The hesitation and displeasure was easy to see, but she put a brave smile on her face. I kissed her long and thoroughly, making sure to pull her soft body up against the hardness of my muscles to make sure our naked images were seared into her brain.

"I'll call you later," I murmured against her lips.

"You better."

"I got you, sweetheart... I love you," I said smoothly.

"I-I love you too, Lo."

I could feel Pretty Girl's eyes on us, but I didn't so much as glance in her direction as I dropped a kiss on Joy's forehead and headed for the door. I could feel Joy's energy reaching out to pull me back into her embrace, but I kept moving purposefully. By the time I'd gotten to the underground garage and hopped into my car, my mind was off of the women upstairs, and it was firmly fixed on the pain that I intended to cause. It took half an hour for me to get to my temporary apartment and another ten minutes for me to grab some clean clothes and my fake passport. The next order of business had me sitting in front of my laptop as I logged into the OnlyFans page that I'd already created, and then I uploaded all of the movies and pictures that I had of Joy and me. When the page was to my liking, I released it to the world and set a forty-eight hour timer on the email bombs that would hit both of her parents with the content simultaneously. Imagining the look on Ant's face as he watched his precious daughter getting slutted out, knowing that the world would see it too, put a huge grin on my face. With that piece of business done, it was time to get on the move. I decided to take my bike in favor of speed and stealth, and then I was back on the road.

By the time I hit the highway, it was a little after 8pm, and by 2am, I was crossing the border into Mexico. At 2:30am, I pulled up in front of my homeboy, Oscar's, house, not at all surprised to find the lights on and music playing loudly from somewhere inside. He was out here in the middle of nowhere, so it wasn't like the neighbors were a factor. By the time I got to his front door, Oscar was pulling it open and opening his arms wide to me.

"My brother from another mother! Get in here!"

Before I could brace for impact, I was wrapped up in a bear hug that made it clear just how much strength and power were harnessed in Oscar's 6'5", three hundred twenty pounds. The muthafucka was built like a tight end.

"If you break my ribs, I'mma break your nose," I said weakly, struggling to get loose from his death grip.

Oscar laughed and gave me a final squeeze before letting my feet touch the earth again.

"It's good to see your new face in person, even though I liked your old face better."

"Truth be told, I did too, but I had to become invisible," I replied, stepping past him into the house.

"I know. Your brother told me right before he told me that I couldn't make a move until you were ready."

I could hear the displeasure in Oscar's voice, and I knew that it was because he didn't like to be told what to do, especially when it came to exercising his right to retaliate against someone in the name of the loyalty that he didn't give freely. Oscar and I had met years ago in prison, and I'd earned that loyalty by shedding blood in his name, so I knew that he'd do anything for me.

"My apologies for the delay, but I'm playing the long game on this one," I said.

"I get it, but I'm glad that it's time to make a move, and I'm assuming that it's gonna be a bloody one given the packages that you had delivered by your brother a few hours ago."

"Where are they?" I asked eagerly.

He motioned for me to follow him, and he led the way down a hallway to a bedroom in the back of his house. When he opened the door, I stepped in to see a man and woman huddled together in a far corner of the room. They had no visible injuries, but I could smell the fear on both of them.

"Good morning. My name is Nathan Ty, and today will be the last day on Earth for the both of you. I pray that you're right with your God."

CHAPTER 13

"How do you want it done?" Oscar asked.

"I want to send an unforgettable message," I replied, still staring coldly at two of the last remaining members of Ant's family.

Without another word, Oscar disappeared from my side and then returned a few minutes later with three more Mexicans just as huge as he was. One man was carrying plastic and an old-fashioned hand saw. Oscar gave them rapid instructions in Spanish while motioning for me to step aside. I moved back out of their way as I pulled my phone out of my pocket in preparation of filming whatever was about to happen.

"I want to take the kill shots myself," I said.

"No problem. We're just gonna remove their hands and feet before we start working on the skin," Oscar replied nonchalantly.

The sounds of a scuffle turned my attention back to what was happening inside the bedroom, and I caught sight of each man choking his captive to sleep. I raised my phone and started filming. The Mexicans made quick work out of the clothes that had been covering Ant's mom and brother, leaving them both naked and stretched out on plastic tarps spread eagle. The legs and arms of both victims were affixed to some type of titanium cord that was tightened on their limbs until it was visibly biting into their skin hard enough to make blood ooze. Once that was accomplished, the opposite ends of the titanium cord were bolted into the floor using an air pressure gun that one of the men had gone to retrieve from somewhere in the house.

"Now the fun begins," Oscar stated, sounding as excited as I felt.

I didn't say a word. I just kept my attention pointed in the same direction that my phone was aimed. I didn't wanna miss a second of the action. They started with Ant's brother first, and although he'd been unconscious, the moment that the saw's blade bit into his right wrist, he came around with screams to announce his return. I felt the smile tugging at the corners of my mouth as I opened my mind and heart to the immeasurable pain that Ant had caused me and my family. The feeling of getting my lick back this way was damn near better than slutting his daughter out. I knew that in the end, the most orgasmic feeling would be to feel Ant's heart stop beating while it was clutched in my bloody palm. The first Mexican managed to cut Darnell's hand clean off before the screaming finally pulled his mother out of her peaceful unconsciousness and into the third realm of hell. When she immediately began to scream, the other Mexican picked up her son's now useless hand and proceeded to smack her repeatedly across the face with it. Oscar and I both laughed hysterically at this, and I made sure to get it all on video. Within the next ten minutes, Darnell lost his other hand, and then his left foot joined the growing pile. By the time the hands and feet of both family members were gone, they'd both succumbed to the pain and passed out again. Little did they know that their torment was far from over.

"Get the blowtorch and the machetes," Oscar ordered.

His men followed instructions without hesitation, returning a few minutes later with the necessary tools. Oscar told them to burn the limbs first so that neither person would bleed out too quickly. When that was done, he ordered them to peel the flesh from each of them like a hunter would a dead deer's skin. It was a captivating two hours later before the work was finished, and Ant's beloved family members were laid out before me looking like chickens that had gotten their muthafuckin feathers plucked.

"You're up," he said, passing me a .44 revolver.

I took it gladly and stepped into the room, still filming with the phone in my left hand. Both of them were barely breathing with their eyes so glassy and glossed over from the unspeakable pain that they'd endured that I doubted that either of them knew where they were.

"If you're wondering why this happened, you can ask Anthony when he joins you in hell. He wanted to up the score, and now the game is officially in overtime," I said.

I shot his brother twice in the face, loving how his blood and brain matter misted onto his mother's face, who was next to die.

"Pl-Please d-don't," she begged.

"Sorry, ma'am. I'm just a worker punching a clock," I replied, pulling the trigger three quick times.

The .44 slugs made her instantly unrecognizable, but I still zoomed in with the camera for a closer look.

"Ohhhh, *Anthonyyyy*, can you come out and *play*?!" I asked in a little kid's sing-song voice. My taunting laughter was the last thing that could be heard before I stopped recording.

"What do you need me to do now?" Oscar asked from behind me.

"Take them both to a public overpass on this side of the border and hang them out for the world to see. Like Chinese lanterns," I replied, slipping my phone back into my pocket as I turned around.

"Not a problem. Anything else?"

"Not right now but thank you for this," I replied genuinely.

"It's nothing. My men needed to have some fun anyway."

Oscar and I smiled at each other, and then I gave him his pistol back before I headed for the front door. The sky was just starting to make its shift in color from deep purple to the lighter lavender that proceeded the orange of the sun's rise. I hopped on my bike and prepared to become one with the wind. By the time that I crossed back into the U.S. and was racing up the West Coast, the sun was making her presence known, and for the first time since my mother died, I actually felt its warmth on my skin. When I pulled over to get gas, I sent the video I'd just made in Tijuana to Bridgette with instructions for her not to upload it until I texted her again. Everything had to be timed just right. I got back on the road and didn't stop until I reached my apartment in San Francisco.

Once I got there, I took a quick shower and changed clothes, grabbed my Ruger 9mm with the built-in beam, and then I jumped in my car to return to Joy's place. It was about 11:30am when I pulled up, and even though I hadn't slept a wink, I wasn't tired in the least bit. I was definitely still running on adrenaline. Before I got out and headed upstairs, I texted Oscar to ask him if the bodies were on display. Within minutes, his response came in the form of a video from the morning news out of Tijuana that showed two bodies suspended from the overpass. It was blamed on the local cartel, but that didn't matter. I sent the video to Bridgette with instructions for her to combine it with the one I'd sent earlier and make it something like a highlight reel. Once she did that, she was to upload it everywhere in ten minutes. She immediately replied with a thumbs up emoji, leaving me nothing left to do except to console the woman upstairs who was anxiously awaiting my return. I grabbed my duffel bag and headed up to Joy's apartment where I let myself in with the key that she'd given me two weeks ago.

"Babe, you here?" I called out.

I heard her bare feet slapping the white marble floor before I saw her, which helped me to brace because she bent the corner at a dead run.

"Oh, my God, *baby!*" she squealed, leaping into the air.

I had just enough time to drop my bag and open my arms before she collided with my chest like an F150 pickup truck. I absorbed her full body weight with only a slight step back, but that left me no time to prepare for her next assault which came in the form of kisses placed all over my face.

"I missed you! I missed you so fucking much! Don't you *ever* do that again," she murmured in between kisses.

I laughed as I carried her into the living room and sat down on the couch with her in my lap.

"Is your mom still here?"

"Nope. And yes, that means you're gonna fuck me *thoroughly* all over this apartment as soon as we finish talking," she replied, working her way with her lips from my face to my neck.

"T-Talk? About what?" I asked, trying to maintain my concentration and deny the primal urges that she was tapping into.

"Just some stuff. It's serious but not in a bad way."

Hearing this pushed the button on my curiosity and gave me the needed strength to halt her seductive onslaught.

"Baby, what's up?" I asked, putting my hands on her shoulders to prevent her continuous attack of kisses.

"Okay, so first, my mom and I talked about you for *hours* after you left, and by the time the conversation was over, she agreed that you were worthy enough to meet my dad. To be completely honest with you, I could give a damn if he doesn't approve or accept our relationship because I'm not letting you go for nothing and nobody. My mom likes the idea of tradition though, so she thinks that you need to meet my dad. What do you think?"

"I'd love to meet your dad, so just tell me when and where," I replied quickly with a genuine smile on my face.

"Really? You would? Oh, my God, I love you!" she squealed, hugging me tightly.

I hugged her back with the same enthusiasm, and as if on cue, the sounds of her phone ringing from its position on the coffee table filled the room. She didn't make a move to answer it, and I didn't suggest it because I knew that this was only the first of many calls.

"So, how do you wanna do this? Do you wanna invite them out to dinner while they're in town? It's convenient, plus I figure that everyone is less likely to show their ass in a public place like a crowded restaurant."

"That's sound logic, but you don't know my father. To say that he's paranoid is putting it lightly, which means that if we go to a restaurant, he'll buy the whole damn place out just for the sake of privacy," she replied.

"Damn... is he in the mob or something?" I asked, feigning slight visible concern.

She laughed at my question while shaking her head no.

"Not hardly, bae, but he's a powerful businessman, and you don't get to be in that position in life without making some equally powerful enemies. Shit, all my dad's cars are bulletproof tanks for real."

I filed that sliver of information away for a later date in case I needed it. I was about to offer up another suggestion to the question of meeting places when the sounds of her notifications going crazy replaced the ringing of her phone. She still ignored it completely, and I didn't utter anything that sounded like a word about it.

"Well, why don't we brainstorm over an early lunch, and you can keep me company in the kitchen while I whip us up something?" I suggested.

"I'm only gonna agree to that because it's proper etiquette that I feed you first and then slut you out."

"Oh, so *you're* gonna slut *me* out, huh?" I asked, dropping my hands to her ass cheeks and gripping them hard enough to make her pussy throb.

"Absolutely. We've gotta catch up because I don't know if you realize it, but last night was the first night since we've been together that we didn't fuck each other to sleep. My pussy and ass were *so* mad at you for leaving us like that."

"I'll beg their forgiveness, but first, I need you to hop off of me so that I can go to the bathroom real quick," I said.

"Or... you could just put that hard dick to use right now," she replied, sliding off my lap and onto her knees in front of me.

Before I could stop her, she'd reached into my pants and pulled my dick out, falling face first on it like she was narcoleptic. Her mouth was so fucking wet and hot that I felt my toes curling involuntarily as she bobbed her head nice and slow. My dick was tapping at the back of her throat until she relaxed her gag reflex, and then, she took me deeper than I'd ever dreamed. Her rhythm was that right verse over a dope beat that made hip hop legendary, and for a second, I was lost to her charms. I almost let myself cum, but I knew that if I did that then we were in for a night of fucking.

"Patience, my love, patience," I said, pulling her greedy mouth up off my dick and bringing her back into my lap.

I sealed my promise with a kiss as I stood up with her

in my arms. I waited until I could feel her heart beating in her lips, and then I tossed her backwards onto the couch.

"Oh, you're gonna pay for teasing me," she vowed, laughing.

I winked at her and headed down the hall to the bathroom. Once I was locked inside, I pulled my phone out and texted Stuckey to let him know that the curtain was about to go up on the final act. No sooner had I slid the phone back into my pocket did I hear Joy's loud, hysterical screams coming from the living room. I made sure to put the proper expression of worry onto my face, and then I rushed from the bathroom.

"Baby, what's wrong? Are you hurt? What is it?" I asked frantically, rushing to her side as she stood in front of the coffee table, clutching her phone.

"My-My-My..."

"Calm down, sweetheart, and just take a deep breath so that you'll be able to talk," I told her.

She nodded her head slowly, and then she pushed her phone into my hand. When I looked down at it, I knew what I would see, and I was prepared to take my expression of shock to the next level, but I never got that far. In the blink of an eye, Joy collapsed too fast for me to catch her, and before I knew it, she was going backwards through the glass coffee table.

"Oh, fuck," I said, seeing blood immediately begin to pool beneath her.

My instincts took over, and my fingers had 911 on the line like the number had been set to speed dial activated by my fingerprints.

"I need help. My girlfriend is hurt and bleeding. She's unconscious, and she fell through a glass table in her living room. We're in the Bay View high rise, 27th floor, apartment 2713. Hurry!" I demanded, disconnecting the call and putting her phone in my pocket.

I knelt down to see if I could find her wound or wounds, but I made sure not to touch her just in case she was impaled by something. I couldn't see a bitch ass thing, which immediately frustrated me. I felt completely helpless in this situation, and that was a feeling that had never sat well with me.

"Think, Nate, think!" I said aloud, looking around the room.

When my eyes landed on her house phone, I quickly crossed the room to it and called down to the front desk. I barely got the explanation out of my mouth before they assured me that someone was on the way up to help. Within minutes, there was a forceful banging on the door, and I ran to open it.

"Where is she?" asked a slim built, Black woman carrying a medical bag of some sort.

"Living room," I replied, stepping aside.

She wasted no time going in that direction, and I was hot on her heels. I wanted to yell at her not to touch her, but I knew that the sane thing to do was to let her work. She took a more thorough inspection than I had, and then, she turned to me.

"I need you to help me lift her. The cuts seem to be coming from her back, and I need to stop the bleeding."

I nodded once, and then we moved to Joy's side.

Looking down into her still face, I felt an unexpected surge of guilt overtake me, and I said a silent prayer that she would be okay. Despite who her father was, she didn't deserve to die.

CHAPTER 14

"Dr. Stefan, is she gonna be alright?" I asked, watching the short, Black woman inspecting Joy's chart in her hand.

"Oh, she'll be fine. All the glass has been removed, and it was really more of a cosmetic injury as opposed to her being dangerously cut."

"It didn't feel cosmetic. It felt like I landed on a spike strip in the middle of the road," Joy said weakly while laying on her side in the hospital bed, facing me.

"I can imagine. You were very lucky though; actually, both of you were lucky," Dr. Stefan said.

"She may have scared me enough to take a few years off my life, Doc, but I was never in any real danger. She was," I replied.

"I didn't mean to scare you, bae. It was just..."

Her sentence trailed off into nothing as she closed her eyes, and a pained expression robbed the ageless beauty from her face. I wanted to tell myself that her back was just hurting her, but my consciousness was whispering the truth of my diabolical planning being the reason that Joy was laid up in the hospital right now. I'd expected and prepared for the crying and her needing to be consoled because that was my intent to make the psychological pull she felt for me that much more unbreakable. I hadn't expected her to pass the fuck out and get hurt though.

"Hey, it's okay, sweetheart," I said, reaching my hand out and taking hers in order to provide comfort.

"Dr. Stefan, why can't I have anything for the pain?" she asked with her eyes still closed and tears staining the starched hospital pillowcase.

"It goes against hospital policy for us to give any type of narcotic pain medication to a woman in her first trimester, so all that we can offer you is more Tylenol. Do you need more now?"

Joy's eyes popped open, and now they were staring into mine as if she was trying to sear a hole in the frontal lobe of my brain. I didn't see fear in her eyes —or even despair at this moment —just a curiosity that let me know that what I'd actually heard the doctor say was what the doctor said.

"F-First trimester? So, that would mean that she-uh-she's pregnant," I stammered, looking up at the doctor.

"According to the bloodwork, she most certainly is, and we ran it three times just to be sure. That's what I meant when I said that you were *both* lucky," Dr. Stefan explained.

"A baby... how do you feel about that, Angelo?" Joy asked, still staring at me.

In my mind, I was clapping my hands and congratulating my sperm swim team because getting her pregnant had been one of the ultimate goals. It was the big payback and the second to last piece of the revenge puzzle.

"I always wanted to be a daddy, so my philosophy is 'the more the merrier'. How do you feel about it?" I asked.

Somehow, my question made her tears spring forward again, but this time, they were accompanied by her dazzling smile.

"I feel like it's a sign from God. It doesn't take away from the tremendous feeling of loss that comes with my uncle and grandma dying, but it fills me with hope for the future. Plus, I'm pregnant by the love of my life," she replied, squeezing my hand tightly.

"Well, congratulations to you both. I'll process your discharge paperwork, and you should be able to go home shortly," Dr. Stefan said before leaving the room.

The sound of a phone ringing suddenly filled the silence, and I reached into my pocket to grab mine. It took me a few seconds to realize that it wasn't my phone ringing though, which made me dig Joy's phone out of my other pocket.

"It says that the call is coming from your mom," I told her.

When she reached out her hand to take it, I passed it to her, and she answered the call. I didn't even need to hear the words to understand that the tone of voice was frantic coming from Pretty Girl. Joy had to immediately take a moment to calm her down, and then it became clear that due to what had happened down in Mexico, Ant had sent a team to get Joy. When they arrived and found nothing except for blood and broken glass, the natural assumption had been that Joy was dead or worse, so Pretty Girl had checked her phone's location. While Joy was explaining to her mom what had happened, I was texting my brother to let him know the same and that I needed a few of his guys to get to the hospital asap. My instincts were telling me that Ant had sent his men this way and that his instructions would've been to retrieve his daughter at all costs. I wasn't about to let her out of my sight though.

"Baby, let me speak to your mom," I said, holding my hand out expectantly toward her.

"Ma, hold on because Angelo wants to talk to you."

When she gave me the phone, I got straight down to bidness.

"Whatever men that you or her father sent to get Joy, you need to tell them to stand down and back off. I will protect her myself," I said.

"That's cute, Angelo, but we prefer to take care of our own. So, if you would please give the phone back to my daughter, I would..."

"You're not hearing me, Diamond. Joy isn't just your family anymore; she's mine too, and I'm gonna be the one to protect her. I advise you to tell your men to go on about their bidness," I said forcefully.

"Just because you two are fucking don't mean that you're family. Now put my daughter back on the phone before I get mad."

I passed Joy the phone back, but it was not because her mother's demands mattered to me in the slightest. The sight of two muscular niggas in dark suits filling the doorway grabbed my attention, and my survival instincts took over from there. Before either man could speak a word or make his intentions clear in any way, my pistol was in my hand, and I upped that bitch like I was playing *Call of Duty*. The beam of red light glowed brightly on the first man's forehead a split second before I squeezed the trigger twice and let his thoughts get some air. His body bounced off of his partner's, pushing the other man into the room with us, but my four well-placed shots knocked his chest through his back and sent him flying back out the open door.

"We gotta go, Joy," I said, rising to my feet while keeping my gun trained on the door. I could hear Pretty Girl yelling something through the phone, but my focus was fixated on what whac-a-mole I could bop next.

"M-Mom, call your men off! I don't care what Dad said. *Call them off!*" she yelled.

I saw a shadow move first, and then a gun barrel came into sight, but I didn't wait for the nigga holding it to bend the corner. I fired two shots at the crack in the door, and I was rewarded with a painful grunt from whoever had just made an uncomfortable landing on the hallway floor.

"Up, Joy, now," I insisted, still keeping my focus on the doorway.

In my peripheral vision, I saw her scrambling out of the bed as fast as her pain would allow, and she immediately grabbed her shorts and shoes. I quickly pulled my t-shirt off and tossed it to her to put on, and then, I picked up the dead man's gun that had flown out of his hand and landed on the floor.

"Take this and stay behind me," I instructed, passing her the pistol before I led the way out of the room.

I took a quick, cautious peek out into the hallway, and then we made a mad dash for the exit stairway that was across from her room. Once I got her in the stairway, I squatted down in front of her.

"Get on my back and hold on tight," I said.

She followed directions, and then I moved as fast as I could down the two flights of stairs that led us out a side door of the building. I didn't stop moving until we'd rounded the corner of the building and arrived at my car in the parking lot. After letting her down so that she could get in, I jumped behind the wheel and got us the fuck out of there like there was a bomb in the building.

"Why did-Why did you shoot them?" she asked, still trying to catch her breath from the physical exertion.

"Because I don't trust them. I don't trust nobody right now and neither should you after what happened to your family."

"But those men worked for my dad, and they were only moving off of my parents' orders," she said, sounding upset.

"I get that, sweetheart, but how do we know that they ain't been compromised? I mean, I'm sure that your dad had men looking after your grandma and uncle too, so that means if somebody got to them then your father's team has a weak link," I reasoned.

My words left her with no immediate response, which was fine by me because I needed to come up with a plan of action real muthafuckin fast. Going back to her place was out of the question and staying at my spot didn't make much sense either. There weren't cameras in the hospital rooms, but there was no doubt that there were cameras in the hallway and stairway that had captured images of our escape. That meant that it was only a matter of time before they figured out who we were.

"We gotta get out of town," I said.

"O-okay, I've got friends in L.A. that we can stay with."

"No, sweetheart, I mean that we need to get out of California altogether because it's the last place that your father and his enemies knew that you were. Predictability ain't our friend right now," I explained.

"I hear you, baby, but my dad is powerful. I mean, the nigga has some real juice in the streets."

"And like you told me before, powerful men come with equally powerful enemies. The average muthafucka couldn't have gotten to your family, so the fact that someone did the horrific shit that they did should prove my point," I pointed out patiently.

"Okay, so where do we go? What do we do?" she asked, raising her voice in frustration.

"First, we're gonna go to my house so that I can grab some shit, and then we're gonna disappear into the night."

"Lo, I can't just disappear on my family. They'll be worried sick, and you don't know my father. He's crazy enough to try and kill you for interfering in family business," she warned.

I chuckled humorlessly at the thought of Ant trying to kill me again, but the image of it gave me a wonderfully bad idea.

"I'll tell your father like I did your mother because that's *my* child you're carrying, and that means you're *my* family to protect. Don't worry though because we'll see your dad soon enough."

"Can I call them at least to let them know that I'm okay? I know that my mama freaked the fuck out after I hung up on her," she said, shaking her head.

"I get it, bae, so go ahead and call them and then drop your phone out the window," I instructed.

"I'm ahead of you on that, love, because I left my phone back at the hospital. I figured that it was how my mama knew where to send the goons."

"Smart girl," I said, passing her my phone.

I saw her dial the number out of the corner of my eye, but then she surprised me by linking the call to my car's Bluetooth and making it a conference call between us and her mother. It only rang twice before I heard Pretty Girl's voice come on the line.

"Mama, why didn't you listen to me and call your men off?"

"I think the better question is why did your nigga shoot first, and who the fuck is he exactly?" she countered.

"I shot because I told you that I'd be the one to protect Joy, but you must not have heard me clearly, so I thought a few bodies dropping would speak your language," I retorted.

"I think that you're confusing your stupidity for bravery, Angelo, because you have *no* idea who my husband is or how far his reach goes. You kidnapping our daughter just sealed your own death in the most painful way you can imagine," she threatened.

"Mama, he didn't kidnap me. I went with him! I love him, and I'm gonna have his baby."

This revelation was met with complete silence, but I could see the look of shocked panic in Pretty Girl's face in my mind's eye, and it made me smile as I reached across the seat to take Joy's hand.

"Are you-Are you saying that you're pregnant?" Pretty Girl asked slowly.

"Yes, Mama, that's what I'm saying, and that's why Angelo is being so protective. It all makes sense now, right?"

"No, no, it don't make sense! You can't be pregnant when you still a baby your damn self, Joy!" she yelled.

"I'm *not* a child nor a baby, and I definitely don't remember you having this same energy when you were passing out your motherly wisdom on how to handle this good ass dick that got me pregnant. What's really the tea?"

"Facts, but I didn't think that I had to tell your stupid ass *not* to get pregnant by a nigga that you just met! You don't know shit about Angelo, other than the fact that he can fuck, so how do you know that he'll be a good dad?"

"Because he's a good man, Ma, and a blind woman can see that shit. Look, I love you, and I love Dad, but this is my life, and I'mma live it to the fullest. My child is a blessing created in love, and fuck anybody who doesn't feel the same way," she replied, tossing my phone out of the open car window.

"Joy, listen, I'm not saying..."

The rest of whatever Pretty Girl had to say was forever lost as the Bluetooth signal dropped, and the car went silent except for the demon under the hood growling as the gears shifted. My hand was still wrapped up in hers, and I gave her fingers a reassuring squeeze to let her know that she wasn't in this alone. Between the two of us, only I knew of the destruction that was still on the horizon, but I'd made up my mind that her and our child wouldn't be the collateral damage that I'd intended initially. I had no idea what our life would look like, but I knew that she wouldn't be left to raise our child alone, and she definitely wouldn't be raising our baby under the dictatorship of Ant. It was time to move the last piece on the board, and then all that would be left was to say that glorious word. Checkmate.

CHAPTER 15

TWO DAYS LATER: VIRGINIA

(Virginia)

"Can you zip my dress up for me?" Joy asked, turning around and giving me an eyeful of her bare back and lace black panties.

I did my best to keep my mind focused on business as I pulled the zipper up, despite the dog in me whistling like an old *Looney Tunes'* cartoon. The funeral for Joy's grandmother and uncle was less than an hour away, so taking our hotel bed for one last spin should've been the last thing on my mind.

"Thank you," she said, turning around to face me.

"You're welcome... are you sure that you're up for this?"

"Do I really have a choice? I mean, I gotta pay my last respects, even if I don't got shit to say to my parents right now," she replied.

"I feel you. I'm just worried about your stress levels

because you know that all that ain't good for the little one you're carrying."

"That's the last time I let your ass stay up all night watching parenting videos with me. But yeah, I know, and that's why you're gonna keep the promise that you made me and have me somewhere tropical by nightfall," she said, smiling wistfully.

"The tickets are paid for."

"Good. Let me go and finish my makeup, and then we can leave for the church," she said, heading toward the bathroom.

I waited until she was inside with the door closed before I reached into the pocket of my slacks and pulled out the burner phone I'd gotten to replace the one she'd scattered across the highway. I called Stuckey and listened to it ring three times before his voice came on the line.

"Sup, bruh?"

"We're leaving for the church in about ten to fifteen minutes. Is shit straight on your end?" I asked.

"Yeah, we've been here for about an hour now, working a twelve-man crew with legit credentials. This shit is gonna go like clockwork."

"Yeah, but only if he doesn't put up a fight," I said, knowing just how probable that scenario was.

"Why would he? He's gotten so arrogant since he went legit that he thinks he's untouchable. I've only spotted about eight men roaming around, trying to blend in despite the fact of the obvious weapons' print bulging from beneath their suits," he said.

"Just make sure to tell your men to keep their head on a

swivel because Pretty Girl is with the shit, and she'll pull a trigger too."

"I hear you loud and clear, bruh. I'll see you in a minute," he replied, disconnecting the call.

I slid the phone back in my pocket and then reached beneath my suit jacket to pull out my Glock .45 with the switch on it to check it one more time. I really didn't wanna shoot this man's mama's funeral up, but thoughts of what happened back at the banquet hall kept invading my mind. The street nigga in me was crying to get his lick back for sure. I'd just finished inspecting my weapon when the bathroom door opened, and Joy reemerged, looking good enough to sin for.

"How do I look? It's not too much is it?" she asked self-consciously.

"There's no such thing as too much, sweetheart, only females that try too hard to do what comes natural to you. You look amazing."

"Thank you. Are you ready?" she asked.

I tucked my gun back into its holster and crossed the room to take her hand.

"I need you to remember that no matter what happens today, I love you and the baby you're carrying," I said seriously.

"Okay... where is this coming from?"

"From the heart. I mean, I know from experience that funerals are never an easy place to be, so I just want you to hold on to what's good in your life right now," I explained.

"That's sweet, baby, and thank you. I don't know what I'd do without you."

"That's not something that you gotta worry about. So... are you ready?" I asked.

"As ready as I can be, I guess."

"Let's go," I said, leading her outside to my car.

The small church in Petersburg, Virginia was only about ten minutes away, but I wanted to do a little recon by driving around the church in order to gauge just how fortified Ant was. A few days ago, that nigga couldn't have imagined anyone shooting up his mother's funeral, but then again, he couldn't actually imagine anyone getting to her either. When Bridgette had posted the video to all social media sites, the shockwave could be felt on other continents. The word savage was used so much that you would've thought that it was a popular new baby name, but the word that me and mine were secretly pushing was *karma*. Blood cried for blood, and now, that nigga, Ant, knew that he wasn't special. I deposited Joy in the passenger seat before going to the driver's side and getting behind the wheel. I pulled my phone out under the pretense of using it for GPS, but really, I just texted Stuckey to let him know that we were on our way. Fifteen minutes later, I pulled up to the back of the building, and it seemed like as soon as we got there, the skies opened up to let the rain free.

"They say that rain at a funeral is a good omen for the dead... What do you think?" she asked, looking over at me.

"I think that anything is possible, but in terms of this particular situation right here, I think that it's safe to say that your loved ones are going to Heaven. Truthfully, they shouldn't even be dead because it's your father that owes the debt in blood."

"A debt? What do you mean?" she asked curiously.

"Nothing, I'm just thinking out loud. Stay right there and I'll get the door for you."

I hopped out before she could say anything or ask me what I truly meant about her dad owing a blood debt. I knew from experience that children had a way of seeing the best in their parents, even when their demons were more obvious than a stop sign. Joy might have been in denial about her dad being the devil, but all truths would set him free today. I opened the door for her and hustled her inside the church before the raindrops could turn her black dress into an after-hours special. The strong smell of roses filled my nose as soon as we crossed the threshold, and the sounds of hushed conversations could be heard throughout the church.

"Let's get you a seat in the back so that you don't have to deal with the crowd," I said.

She nodded okay and let me take her arm to guide her out into the main hall of the church to find her a pew. The crowd was almost to capacity already, but we had half of the very back pew to ourselves. No sooner had we sat down though, I caught sight of Ant and Pretty Girl headed in our direction with four men in tow.

"We've got company," I mumbled out of the side of my mouth.

Joy looked at me and then followed the direction that my eyes had taken before she reached for my hand and locked her fingers through mine.

"Joy, come with me," Pretty Girl demanded.

"For what, Ma?"

"Just do as your mother says and let me have a talk wit your little friend," Ant said.

"He's not my friend, Daddy; he's my man... and the father to my unborn child."

"Yeah, your mama told me that you were out here on some *thot* shit, but you won't be having no babies. Not right now and *not* by this nigga," Ant declared.

"You can't make me abort my baby!" Joy said heatedly, raising her voice enough to make heads turn.

"Oh, I can't? Well, you can either go to the doctors and let them take care of it, or I can blow that little muthafucka out of your back," Ant threatened, pulling his pistol out.

Gasps echoed throughout the church, but no one said a word to try and stop his madness.

"Ant, put the fucking gun down," Pretty Girl said, stepping in front of him.

I seized the moment of her shielding us to pull my own gun out, stand up so that Joy was behind me, and level that muthafucka at Ant's face right over top of Pretty Girl's head.

"You still ain't learned about fucking with a nigga's family, huh, Lamborghini?" I asked.

My usage of his street name caught him off guard, causing him to squint at me curiously.

"What did you call me?" he asked.

"You heard me clearly, nigga, but you're trying to figure out how I know you because I don't look familiar. It's because modern medicine allows for optical illusions," I replied, smiling broadly.

"Modern medicine wouldn't cause me to forget a face... unless..."

"I can smell the wood burning and see the wheels turning, Anthony, so that ten-million-dollar question is, which one of your enemies am I?" I asked.

"An-Angelo, what are you talking about?" Joy asked from behind me.

I ignored her question and watched the transition on Ant's face morph from disbelief to absolute fear of the unknown.

"Diamond, why don't you tell him who I really am?" I suggested.

She spun around to face me, and I could see the intent to curse my very existence building up within her eyes, but then there was a sudden shift that left her stare blank.

"It don't really matter who the fuck you are because you'll never make it out of here alive," Ant vowed.

"I beg to differ, but we'll get to the climactic finish in due time. For now, let's just solve the first riddle of the man beneath this gorgeous face. I'm the same man that sent your nephew and cousin into the afterlife in the express lane," I said, smiling with vindication.

"Oh, God-Oh, God, no," Pretty Girl said, dropping to her knees as if she meant to pray right there in between Anthony and I.

Surprisingly, his expression remained neutral, almost as if he didn't hear my declaration, or he didn't believe it.

"Big bad Nate Dog. You know, I'm not actually that surprised, although I admit that I didn't exactly see this coming. I guess it's a good thing that I learned a long time ago that playing chess meant being ten moves ahead of your opponent," Ant said.

His statement confused me at first, and then he looked

to his left and gave some type of signal. Suddenly, there was movement in the pews toward the front of the church and out stepped my sister, Yah Yah, followed by two more men. I did my best to mask my shock at seeing her, but I knew that I was failing because I could feel my mouth hanging open.

"Yah Yah. are you okay?" I asked when she stopped beside Ant.

"Is she okay? Damn, my nigga, you really are slow, huh? I mean, you still ain't figured it out that your own sister was the one who fed you to Flacco?" Ant asked.

I opened my mouth to call bullshit, despite my earlier belief of the same conspiracy theory, but the look on Yah Yah's face rendered my words completely unnecessary.

"With that being the case, then you must realize that she's no good as leverage to use against me," I said.

"You're absolutely right... but she is useful in upping the score," he replied.

Before I could flinch, he raised his pistol and shot Yah Yah in the temple. It felt like the whole church moaned when my sister's body hit the floor, but I was left with nothing but astonishment and shock. I didn't even get a chance to react before Stuckey and his men moved on Ant.

They threw him to the floor, and I was envisioning me blowing his brains out like he'd just done my baby sister, but my thoughts couldn't organize. The disbelief clouding my mind had me thinking that if I moved quick enough, I could somehow scoop Yah Yah's brains back into her skull, but I made no move to try it. The arm holding my pistol out in front of me dropped to my side, and the feeling of extreme exhaustion swept over me.

"Lo, what the fuck just happened?" Joy asked, suddenly appearing beside me.

"Joy, you get the fuck away from him," Pretty Girl growled, springing to her feet.

"Ma, you can't keep us apart!"

"Let them be together, Diamond... nothing in this world would make me happier," Ant said before he was hauled away in handcuffs.

"I need you to take Joy and get her out of here, bruh," Stuckey said, pushing me backwards gently.

"Joy, you don't understand. You *can't* be with him!" Pretty Girl insisted, sounding almost hysterical.

Joy didn't say a word. She simply slipped her hand into mine and pulled me back toward the side door that we'd entered through. The sounds of Pretty Girl screaming her daughter's name was the last thing I heard from inside the church before I was back outside in the rain. We hopped in the car and pulled off in silence, but I knew that wouldn't last long.

"I need you to explain to me what the fuck just happened, who you really are, and why my father just executed a woman at my grandmother's and uncle's funeral."

"It's... complicated," I replied.

"Well, un-fucking-complicate it! None of this shit makes sense, but something tells me that I just got fucked and not in a good way!"

"Calm down, Joy, the baby..."

"I *don't* fucking need you to remind me that I'm pregnant, nigga!" she screamed.

As badly as I wanted to calm her down, I knew that

either path that I chose would yield the same results of borderline hysteria. I'd known that this day was inevitable, but now that it was here, I just wanted to push it into the farthest corners of my mind.

"Do you remember about seven months ago when two people got killed on IG Live during an attempted robbery?" I asked.

"Yeah, why?"

"I was the man who killed them," I stated pointedly.

"No, you weren't because he's dead and... Wait, that's what you meant back at the church when you said that you had a new face. Y-You're Nathan Ty?"

Before I could answer or try to explain, my phone started ringing, and it startled both of us because it must've connected to the car's Bluetooth once I'd gotten back inside. It was a welcome distraction nonetheless, and I answered without hesitation.

"Yo?"

"Bruh, turn the car around."

"Stuckey?" I asked, surprised.

"Yeah, it's me. Now turn the car around and bring Joy back because you can't go anywhere with her."

"Why not?" I asked, getting a bad feeling.

"Listen, I'll explain everything once you get back here, but you gotta turn the car around now, Nate," he insisted, sounding more panicked by the second.

I trusted my brother with my life, but something was telling me that turning this car around wasn't my best move.

"Look, bruh, we need a minute to talk and figure some shit out, so I'll just call you whenever..."

"No, goddammit! Bring her back now!" he yelled.

"Why, nigga?!" I yelled back.

"Because she's not Anthony's biological daughter, and that nigga knew that."

"Okay, so fucking what?" I asked, not grasping the importance of the news.

"Do the math, genius! If Joy ain't Ant's biological daughter, and the only nigga that Pretty Girl was fucking was you, then that means..."

"That y-y-you're my father," Joy whispered, looking at me in horror.

"Oh... my... God."

2 BE CONTINUED...

LOCK DOWN PUBLICATIONS AND CA$H PRESENTS

ASSISTED PUBLISHING PACKAGES

BASIC PACKAGE

$498

Editing

Cover Design

Formatting

UPGRADED PACKAGE

$800

Typing

Editing

Cover Design

Formatting

ADVANCE PACKAGE

$1,200

Typing

Editing

Cover Design

Formatting

Copyright registration

Proofreading

Upload book to Amazon

LDP SUPREME PACKAGE

$1,500

Typing

Editing

Cover Design

Formatting

Copyright registration

Proofreading

Set up Amazon account

Upload book to Amazon

Advertise on LDP, Amazon and Facebook Page

Submission Guidelines

Submit the first three chapters of your completed manuscript to ldpsubmissions@gmail.com. In the subject line add Your Book's Title. The manuscript must be in a Word Doc file and sent as an attachment. Document should be in Times New Roman, double spaced, and in size 12 font. Also, provide your synopsis and full contact information. If sending multiple submissions, they must each be in a separate email.

Have a story but no way to send it electronically? You can still submit to LDP/Ca$h Presents. Send in the first three chapters, written or typed, of your completed manuscript to:

LDP: Submissions Dept
P.O. Box 944
Stockbridge, GA 30281-9998

DO NOT send original manuscript. Must be a duplicate.
Provide your synopsis and a cover letter containing your full contact information.

Thanks for considering LDP and Ca$h Presents.

NEW RELEASES

BLOODLINE OF A SAVAGE 1&2
THESE VICIOUS STREETS 1&2
RELENTLESS GOON
RELENTLESS GOON 2
BY PRINCE A. TAUHID

THE BUTTERFLY MAFIA 1-3
BY FUMIYA PAYNE

A THUG'S STREET PRINCESS 1&2
BY MEESHA

CITY OF SMOKE 2
BY MOLOTTI

STEPPERS 1,2&3
THE REAL BADDIES OF CHI-RAQ
BY KING RIO

. . .

THE LANE 1&2
BY KEN-KEN SPENCE

THUG OF SPADES 1&2
LOVE IN THE TRENCHES 2
CORNER BOYS
BY COREY ROBINSON

TIL DEATH 3
BY ARYANNA

THE BIRTH OF A GANGSTER 4
BY DELMONT PLAYER

PRODUCT OF THE STREETS 1&2
BY DEMOND "MONEY" ANDERSON

NO TIME FOR ERROR
BY KEESE

. . .

MONEY HUNGRY DEMONS
BY TRANAY ADAMS

STANDING ON HER BUSINESS 2
BY DG SANTANA

TENDER
BY KHUFU

HUB CITY MENACE
BY JAQUILLE M. WHITE

COUNTDOWN TO A KILLA
CLOCK'S TICKING
BY LO-LIFE

DYING FOR LIKES
KILLING AIN'T A GAME
BY ARYANNA

Coming Soon from Lock Down Publications/Ca$h Presents

IF YOU CROSS ME ONCE 6
ANGEL V
By Anthony Fields

IMMA DIE BOUT MINE 5
By Aryanna

A THUGS STREET PRINCESS 3
By Meesha

PRODUCT OF THE STREETS 3
By Demond Money Anderson

CORNER BOYS 2
By Corey Robinson

THE MURDER QUEENS 6&7
By Michael Gallon

CITY OF SMOKE 3
By Molotti

CONFESSIONS OF A DOPE BOY
By Nicholas Lock

THA TAKEOVER
By Keith Chandler

BETRAYAL OF A G 2
By Ray Vinci

CRIME BOSS
By Playa Ray

Available Now

. . .

RESTRAINING ORDER 1 & 2
By CA$H & Coffee

LOVE KNOWS NO BOUNDARIES 1-3
By Coffee

RAISED AS A GOON I, II, III & IV
BRED BY THE SLUMS I, II, III
BLAST FOR ME I & II
ROTTEN TO THE CORE I II III
A BRONX TALE I, II, III
DUFFLE BAG CARTEL I II III IV V VI
HEARTLESS GOON I II III IV V
A SAVAGE DOPEBOY I II
DRUG LORDS I II III
CUTTHROAT MAFIA I II
KING OF THE TRENCHES
By Ghost

LAY IT DOWN I & II
LAST OF A DYING BREED I II
BLOOD STAINS OF A SHOTTA I & II III
By Jamaica

. . .

LOYAL TO THE GAME I II III
LIFE OF SIN I, II III
By TJ & Jelissa

IF LOVING HIM IS WRONG…I & II
LOVE ME EVEN WHEN IT HURTS I II III
By Jelissa

PUSH IT TO THE LIMIT
By Bre' Hayes

BLOODY COMMAS I & II
SKI MASK CARTEL I, II & III
KING OF NEW YORK I II, III IV V
RISE TO POWER I II III
COKE KINGS I II III IV V
BORN HEARTLESS I II III IV
KING OF THE TRAP I II
By T.J. Edwards

WHEN THE STREETS CLAP BACK I & II III

THE HEART OF A SAVAGE I II III IV
MONEY MAFIA I II
LOYAL TO THE SOIL I II III
By Jibril Williams

A DISTINGUISHED THUG STOLE MY HEART I
II & III
LOVE SHOULDN'T HURT I II III IV
RENEGADE BOYS 1-4
PAID IN KARMA 1-3
SAVAGE STORMS 1-3
AN UNFORESEEN LOVE 1-3
BABY, I'M WINTERTIME COLD 1-3
A THUG'S STREET PRINCESS 1&2
By Meesha

A GANGSTER'S CODE 1-3
A GANGSTER'S SYN 1-3
THE SAVAGE LIFE 1-3
CHAINED TO THE STREETS 1-3
BLOOD ON THE MONEY 1-3
A GANGSTA'S PAIN 1-3
BEAUTIFUL LIES AND UGLY TRUTHS
CHURCH IN THESE STREETS
By J-Blunt

CUM FOR ME 1-8
An LDP Erotica Collaboration

BLOOD OF A BOSS 1-5
SHADOWS OF THE GAME
TRAP BASTARD
By Askari

THE STREETS BLEED MURDER 1-3
THE HEART OF A GANGSTA 1-3
By Jerry Jackson

WHEN A GOOD GIRL GOES BAD
By Adrienne

THE COST OF LOYALTY 1-3
By Kweli

BRIDE OF A HUSTLA 1-3
THE FETTI GIRLS 1-3
CORRUPTED BY A GANGSTA 1-4

BLINDED BY HIS LOVE
THE PRICE YOU PAY FOR LOVE 1-3
DOPE GIRL MAGIC 1-3
By Destiny Skai

A KINGPIN'S AMBITION
A KINGPIN'S AMBITION II
I MURDER FOR THE DOUGH
By Ambitious

TRUE SAVAGE 1-7
DOPE BOY MAGIC 1-3
MIDNIGHT CARTEL 1-3
CITY OF KINGZ 1&2
NIGHTMARE ON SILENT AVE
THE PLUG OF LIL MEXICO 1&2
CLASSIC CITY
By Chris Green

A GANGSTER'S REVENGE 1-4
THE BOSS MAN'S DAUGHTERS 1-5
A SAVAGE LOVE 1&2
BAE BELONGS TO ME 1&2
A HUSTLER'S DECEIT 1-3
WHAT BAD BITCHES DO 1-3

SOUL OF A MONSTER 1-3
KILL ZONE
A DOPE BOY'S QUEEN 1-3
TIL DEATH 1-3
IMMA DIE BOUT MINE 1-4
By Aryanna

A DOPEBOY'S PRAYER
By Eddie "Wolf" Lee

THE KING CARTEL 1-3
By Frank Gresham

THESE NIGGAS AIN'T LOYAL 1-3
By Nikki Tee

GANGSTA SHYT 1-3
By CATO

THE ULTIMATE BETRAYAL
By Phoenix

. . .

BOSS'N UP 1-3
By Royal Nicole

I LOVE YOU TO DEATH
By Destiny J

I RIDE FOR MY HITTA
I STILL RIDE FOR MY HITTA
By Misty Holt

LOVE & CHASIN' PAPER
By Qay Crockett

TO DIE IN VAIN
SINS OF A HUSTLA
By ASAD

BROOKLYN HUSTLAZ
By Boogsy Morina

. . .

BROOKLYN ON LOCK 1 & 2
By Sonovia

GANGSTA CITY
By Teddy Duke

A DRUG KING AND HIS DIAMOND 1-3
A DOPEMAN'S RICHES
HER MAN, MINE'S TOO 1&2
CASH MONEY HO'S
THE WIFEY I USED TO BE 1&2
PRETTY GIRLS DO NASTY THINGS
By Nicole Goosby

LIPSTICK KILLAH 1-3
CRIME OF PASSION 1-3
FRIEND OR FOE 1-3
By Mimi

TRAPHOUSE KING 1-3
KINGPIN KILLAZ 1-3

STREET KINGS 1&2
PAID IN BLOOD 1&2
CARTEL KILLAZ 1-3
DOPE GODS 1&2
By Hood Rich

THE STREETS ARE CALLING
By Duquie Wilson

STEADY MOBBN' 1-3
THE STREETS STAINED MY SOUL 1-3
By Marcellus Allen

WHO SHOT YA 1-3
SON OF A DOPE FIEND 1-4
HEAVEN GOT A GHETTO 1&2
SKI MASK MONEY 1&2
By Renta

GORILLAZ IN THE BAY 1-4
TEARS OF A GANGSTA 1/&2
3X KRAZY 1&2
STRAIGHT BEAST MODE 1&2

By DE'KARI

TRIGGADALE 1-3
MURDA WAS THE CASE 1-3
By Elijah R. Freeman

SLAUGHTER GANG 1-3
RUTHLESS HEART 1-3
By Willie Slaughter

GOD BLESS THE TRAPPERS 1-3
THESE SCANDALOUS STREETS 1-3
FEAR MY GANGSTA 1-5
THESE STREETS DON'T LOVE NOBODY 1-2
BURY ME A G 1-5
A GANGSTA'S EMPIRE 1-4
THE DOPEMAN'S BODYGAURD 1&2
THE REALEST KILLAZ 1-3
THE LAST OF THE OGS 1-3
By Tranay Adams

MARRIED TO A BOSS 1-3
By Destiny Skai & Chris Green

. . .

KINGZ OF THE GAME 1-7
CRIME BOSS 1-3
By Playa Ray

FUK SHYT
By Blakk Diamond

DON'T F#CK WITH MY HEART 1&2
By Linnea

ADDICTED TO THE DRAMA 1-3
IN THE ARM OF HIS BOSS
By Jamila

LOYALTY AIN'T PROMISED 1&2
By Keith Williams

YAYO 1-4
A SHOOTER'S AMBITION 1&2

BRED IN THE GAME
By S. Allen

TRAP GOD 1-3
RICH $AVAGE 1-3
MONEY IN THE GRAVE 1-3
CARTEL MONEY
By Martell Troublesome Bolden

FOREVER GANGSTA 1&2
GLOCKS ON SATIN SHEETS 1&2
By Adrian Dulan

TOE TAGZ 1-4
LEVELS TO THIS SHYT 1&2
IT'S JUST ME AND YOU
By Ah'Million

KINGPIN DREAMS 1-3
RAN OFF ON DA PLUG
By Paper Boi Rari

THE STREETS MADE ME 1-3
By Larry D. Wright

CONFESSIONS OF A GANGSTA 1-4
CONFESSIONS OF A JACKBOY 1-3
CONFESSIONS OF A HITMAN
By Nicholas Lock

I'M NOTHING WITHOUT HIS LOVE
SINS OF A THUG
TO THE THUG I LOVED BEFORE
A GANGSTA SAVED XMAS
IN A HUSTLER I TRUST
By Monet Dragun

QUIET MONEY 1-3
THUG LIFE 1-3
EXTENDED CLIP 1&2
A GANGSTA'S PARADISE
By Trai'Quan

CAUGHT UP IN THE LIFE 1-3
THE STREETS NEVER LET GO 1-3

By Robert Baptiste

NEW TO THE GAME 1-3
MONEY, MURDER & MEMORIES 1-3
By Malik D. Rice

CREAM 2-3
THE STREETS WILL TALK
By Yolanda Moore

THE STREETS WILL NEVER CLOSE 1-3
By K'ajji

LIFE OF A SAVAGE 1-4
A GANGSTA'S QUR'AN 1-4
MURDA SEASON 1-3
GANGLAND CARTEL 1-3
CHI'RAQ GANGSTAS 1-4
KILLERS ON ELM STREET 1-3
JACK BOYZ N DA BRONX 1-3
A DOPEBOY'S DREAM 1-3
JACK BOYS VS DOPE BOYS 1-3
COKE GIRLZ

COKE BOYS
SOSA GANG 1&2
BRONX SAVAGES
BODYMORE KINGPINS
BLOOD OF A GOON
By Romell Tukes

CONCRETE KILLA 1-3
VICIOUS LOYALTY 1-3
By Kingpen

THE ULTIMATE SACRIFICE 1-6
KHADIFI
IF YOU CROSS ME ONCE 1-3
ANGEL 1-4
IN THE BLINK OF AN EYE
By Anthony Fields

THE LIFE OF A HOOD STAR
By Ca$h & Rashia Wilson

NIGHTMARES OF A HUSTLA 1-3
BLOOD AND GAMES 1&2

By King Dream

GHOST MOB
By Stilloan Robinson

HARD AND RUTHLESS 1&2
MOB TOWN 251
THE BILLIONAIRE BENTLEYS 1-3
REAL G'S MOVE IN SILENCE
By Von Diesel

MOB TIES 1-7
SOUL OF A HUSTLER, HEART OF A KILLER 1-3
GORILLAZ IN THE TRENCHES
By SayNoMore

BODYMORE MURDERLAND 1-3
THE BIRTH OF A GANGSTER 1-4
By Delmont Player

FOR THE LOVE OF A BOSS 1&2

By C. D. Blue

KILLA KOUNTY 1-5
By Khufu

MOBBED UP 1-4
THE BRICK MAN 1-5
THE COCAINE PRINCESS 1-10
STEPPERS 1-3
SUPER GREMLIN 1-4
By King Rio

MONEY GAME 1&2
By Smoove Dolla

A GANGSTA'S KARMA 1-4
By FLAME

KING OF THE TRENCHES 1-3
By GHOST & TRANAY ADAMS

. . .

QUEEN OF THE ZOO 1&2
By Black Migo

GRIMEY WAYS 1-3
BETRAYAL OF A G
By Ray Vinci

XMAS WITH AN ATL SHOOTER
By Ca$h & Destiny Skai

KING KILLA 1&2
By Vincent "Vitto" Holloway

BETRAYAL OF A THUG 1&2
By Fre$h

THE MURDER QUEENS 1-5
By Michael Gallon

. . .

FOR THE LOVE OF BLOOD 1-4
By Jamel Mitchell

HOOD CONSIGLIERE 1&2
NO TIME FOR ERROR
By Keese

PROTÉGÉ OF A LEGEND 1&2
LOVE IN THE TRENCHES 1&2
By Corey Robinson

THE PLUG'S RUTHLESS DAUGHTER
By Tony Daniels

BORN IN THE GRAVE 1-3
CRIME PAYS
By Self Made Tay

MOAN IN MY MOUTH

By XTASY

TORN BETWEEN A GANGSTER AND A
GENTLEMAN
By J-BLUNT & Miss Kim

LOYALTY IS EVERYTHING 1-3
CITY OF SMOKE 1&2
By Molotti

HERE TODAY GONE TOMORROW 1&2
By Fly Rock

WOMEN LIE MEN LIE 1-4
FIFTY SHADES OF SNOW 1-3
STACK BEFORE YOU SPLURGE
GIRLS FALL LIKE DOMINOES
NAÏVE TO THE STREETS
By ROY MILLIGAN

PILLOW PRINCESS

By S. Hawkins

THE BUTTERFLY MAFIA 1-3
SALUTE MY SAVAGERY 1&2
By Fumiya Payne

THE LANE 1&2
By Ken-Ken Spence

THE PUSSY TRAP 1-5
By Nene Capri

DIRTY DNA
By Blaque

SANCTIFIED AND HORNY
by XTASY

www.ingramcontent.com/pod-product-compliance
Lightning Source LLC
Chambersburg PA
CBHW070514260626
47161CB00004B/1548